NaNoWriMo 2021 A.

TIMELINES
OF THE
CHRONOGARCHY

ALFRED LAMBREMONT WEBRE, JD, MEd

National Novel Writing Month

WINNER

is proud to certify

Alfred Lambremont Webre, JD, MEd

author of

TIMELINES OF THE CHRONOGARCHY

This month, you wrote a novel. You wrote that novel with a community of hundreds of thousands of writers around the world. You contributed to the millions of words we wrote collectively: imagining and creating, exploring joy and heartbreak, laughter and pain. As James Baldwin once said, "It was books that taught me that the things that tormented me most were the very things that connected me with all the people who were alive, who had ever been alive." Thank you for being a part of this connected creative community. Congratulations on your incredible accomplishment.

TIM KIM
Program Director

MARYA BRENNAN
Program Director

GRANT FAULKER
Executive Director

November 12, 2021

WIN DATE

Alfred Lambremont Webre,
JD, MEd, CERT Public Health

NaNoWriMo.org Winner

2021

2022AD Positive Timeline for Earth Human Souls — Ascending

Time is an engine driving events and meaning, ponders Sophie. She scrolls down a 24-page sample on her pampered 27-inch iMac desktop. Kindle downloads bright color Cover, Frontispiece, Title Page, Table of Contents. Sophie was born Sophia, a parental tribute to the Goddess of Wisdom. Wisdom is a focus of Sophie's life as informed, awakened, blogging, vlogging journalist, and free Soul. Is Sophie 30 years old? Is she 50 going on 70, an Elder in hiding? Colleagues, friends, and lovers alike wondered at Sophie's timeless presence.

One fragment of the Frontispiece jumps to Sophie's attention as she scrolls:

Chronogarchy —
Neologism Meaning
"Those Who Rule Through Time"

Sophie's mind rested on: "Those Who Rule Through Time". Does that mean 'those who use the Dimension of Time to Rule', she wondered?

Briskly opening a new tab in her Brave browser, Sophie ran a DuckDuckGo search on "Neologism" at the Free Dictionary. In her careful manner, she studied "Neologism's" varied and polarized meanings:

neologism

Also found in: Thesaurus, Medical, Encyclopedia, Wikipedia.

ne·ol·o·gism (nē-ŏl′ə-jĭz′əm, nē′ō-lō′-)

n.

1. A new word, expression, or usage.
2. The creation or use of new words or senses.
3. Psychology
    a. The invention of new words regarded as a symptom of certain psychotic disorders, such as schizophrenia.
    b. A word so invented.
4. Theology A new doctrine or a new interpretation of scripture.
   ne·ol′o·gist n.
   ne·ol′o·gis′tic, ne·ol′o·gis′ti·cal adj.

Usage Note: The traditional pronunciation of neologism is accented on the second syllable (nē-ŏl′ə-jĭz′əm). In our 2015 survey, this is the pronunciation preferred by 72 percent of the Usage Panel. A newer variant pronunciation accented on the third syllable (nē′ō-lō′jĭz′əm) is preferred by 28 percent of the Panel; however, only half of the Panel finds it acceptable.

neologism (nɪˈɒləˌdʒɪzəm) or neology

n, pl -gisms or -gies

1. (Linguistics) a newly coined word, or a phrase or familiar word used in a new sense
2. (Linguistics) the practice of using or introducing neologisms
3. rare a tendency towards adopting new views, esp rationalist views, in matters of religion
   [C18: via French from neo- + -logism, from Greek logos word, saying]
   neˈologist n
   neˌoloˈgistic, neˌoloˈgistical, neological adj
   neˌoloˈgistically, ˌneoˈlogically adv

n.

1. a new word or phrase or an existing word used in a new sense.
2. the introduction or use of new words or new senses of existing words.
3. a word invented and understood only by the speaker, occurring most often in the speech of schizophrenics.
   [1790–1800; < French néologisme]
   ne•ol′o•gist, n.
   ne•ol`o•gis′tic, adj.
   ne•ol′o•gize`, v.i. -gized, -giz•ing.

1. a new word, usage, or phrase.

2. the coining or introduction of new words or new senses for established words. See also theology. — neologian, neologist, n. — neologistic, neologistical, adj.

neologism

1. A word or expression that is newly created.

2. A newly coined word or expression.[1]

An unusual event in Sophie's life as an indie journalist, blogger, and vlogger was unfolding in this moment of time. Sophie had never heard or seen the term "Chronogarchy" before. Intrigued, surprised, Sophie wanted to test the value of this unknown word.

Sophie exercises due caution around these dictionary words on the large iMac screen dominating the writing desk in the spare bedroom she converted into a Broadcast and Author's Studio in her house. Words are a journalist's tools, medium of exchange, and barter with the world at large. The value of a journalist can depend on the value of the words a journalist uses.

One branch of the polarized meaning of "Neologism" felt clear. Sophie prided herself on the depth of her personal command of language — at least of the English and Spanish languages. With Google Translate and 10 other free translation apps, she felt control over Earth's linguistic Tower of Babel.

1. A word or expression that is newly created.

2. A newly coined word or expression.

Another etymological branch of the meaning of "Neologism" was troubling to Sophie, and she pushed further into it:

3. a word invented and understood only by the speaker, occurring most often in the speech of schizophrenics.

3. Psychology

a. The invention of new words regarded as a symptom of certain psychotic disorders, such as schizophrenia

The grounded indie journalist mind in Sophie asked itself: How stable and sound are the concepts behind the "Chronogarchy"? Is the "Chronogarchy" another catch-all for the mentally ill to posit delusionary concepts about the control of human society through Time?

"How come I have never heard of Chronogarchy, even the word itself!? Let's run an online vetting right now of 'Chronogarchy'", thought Sophie aloud, her journalist caution feelers now activated. "I want to see whether 'Chronogarchy' is really a neologism — a newly invented or coined word, a fragment of schizophrenia, or a research and marketing scam?"

On her trusted iMac, Sophie opens a new Brave tab and goes to DuckDuckGo, her favorite search engine at the moment in an ever-shifting online arena.

Ever since Alphabet took over Google and You Tube, Google has maintained 92% of the Internet search market. Google's Gmail, which Sophie uses as a convenient online email platform to bundle her various email accounts, had started sending Sophie's important mail to SPAM. Alphabet's Google's You Tube had targeted her videos in pre-emptive strikes, almost deplatforming her as a vlogger.

Vimeo, where she had a professional paid account and Bitchute, the darling of a naïve Truth Movement branch of the Truth movement, had both ruthlessly closed her vlogging accounts during a wild week following Sophie's reporting on how an Earth-like human inhabited planet in our solar system became the Asteroid Belt following a Reptilian-Human Planetary Nuclear War 750,000 years ago that also made Mars, another Earth-like human inhabited planet, an obloid sphere in space with no vegetation, little atmosphere, Reptoid dinosaurs roaming the surface, and one million Mars human survivors in cities underground.

Sophie's professional vlogging is now migrated to Odysee, New Tube, Brighteon, and Rumble. Ever the quick-eyed reporter, Sophie now wants to know if the "Chronogarchy" is an authentic news lead. Is the "Chronogarchy" a true sanity-based neologism with value and replicable research content that Sophie can a roll-out with success and social benefit to the demanding journalistic beats she covers and skeptical audiences she serves? Who says women journalists are second-rate?

At DuckDuckGo, Sophie enters "Chronogarchy" in quotes to eliminate all but exacting search results.[2]

One of the earliest search results Sophie finds is dated July 29, 2016, where the lawyer, this time identified as "Zofyo Arni ", is on a Panel and speaks about the "Chronogarchy".[3]

GoldFish Report ExoPolitics RoundTable Part 3 "Manifesting Our New Society"
With the Ambassador of the Red Dragon Family, COBRA, Zofyo Arni, and Capt. Max Steel
July 29, 2016

LOUISA — *"Some of us have this to a certain degree. A lot of people say 'I knew someone was going to call before they called' or 'I just knew something' and you don't know how you knew it, but you just knew it. Zofyo, you were talking about your book before and I know you have had your own interesting experiences. But Zofyo Arni we can develop this and as Cobra said this Veil needs to come down. What can you tell us about that?*

"Zofyo? As Cobra reported, does that mean this veil is thinning or that there are holes in it or is there a meshing occurring and disintegrating? What does that mean?"

ZOFYO — *"Yes, that is a very interesting question. We are all monitoring it to see. I call a particular piece of it the* **Chronogarchy** *because it used a particular technology which is secret time travel technology. Secret teleportation and time travel technology since we live in a time-space hologram, time just being one of the dimensions of height, width, depth, and time space, then you can dial up any position in our time space hologram and teleport there, essentially. I can very quickly describe for the audience what we* *have been able to document using the law of evidence which is good enough for courts and that is eyewitness documentary evidence, what we have on the record. I have exhibit A here, my book ExoPolitics that supposedly founded the science of ExoPolitics. It was written in Vancouver here in 1999, it was published online as a free e-book to change the paradigm, it was published as a soft cover in 2005, and it was promptly time traveled by secret CIA time travel technology back to the year we know at least nineteen sixty-six. Because I had a meeting with Governor Winthrop Rockefeller, a private meeting with only two other people there at Yale Law School in nineteen sixty-six because he had this, he gang stalked me. And then the chrononaut Alexander Uine witnessed this as part of project Pegasus in nineteen seventy-one in the company of two other people including his father who was part of the CIA time travel project and in nineteen seventy-one I was general counsel of the Department of Environmental Protection Administration in New York City. I was invited to a meeting at what later proved to be around fifty Department of Defense and CIA time travel officers who had been briefed on my book. They wanted to see what I looked like in nineteen seventy-one because they knew that on July 29, 2016, I would be a whistle blower saying, they control time and they are a **Chronogarchy** and I'm blowing the whistle along with a whole army of whistle blowers and this is how to get to the future successfully. So now, that's a real piece of evidence that's Exhibit A." [Search added Bold]*

Another of the earliest search results for "Chronogarchy" that Sophie finds is dated October 30, 2016, a You Tube interview with the same lawyer, now named "Zofyo Arni " who for one hour and six minutes is interviewed on Revolution Radio by host Mark Snyder of Ohio Exopolitics and says the following about "Chronogarchy".[4]

The Clinton-Bush-CIA Chrono-garchy uses Artificial Intelligence to manipulate humanity

Zofyo Arni interviews :
- *Michael Savage has recently been kicked off the air.*
- *9/11/2016- After Hillary Collapsed, body double. Any Legal Issues with using body double for a Candidate? Public officers can use them but can a Candidate use a body double? Is that false advertising? Using a body double for a Candidate is likely a mis-representation and violation of electoral codes. (Ed. Note: HILLARY CLINTON is a public office. Any BODY can "step into" the insurance franchise. Attorneys "step into the legally incompetent artificial person" as standard practice.)*
- *Law and Order has broken down in the UNITED STATES, INC. It's a Chronocracy Tyranny.*
- *The Hidden Shadow Time Travel Government. Time Travel Pirates. They have access to and control over time travel technology. Using it to manipulate the political and governmental machinery. US Presidency has been usurped by pre-selection. Since Bush I, presidents have been identified and groomed by the Shadow Pirates.*
- *November 8th, 2016 Elections. Shadow Time Travel Pirates have known since 1971 from time travel programs the Future Presidents. Alexander Uine running for President to disclose Time Technology. It's being run from some place in time-space, but we don't know where-when; from the future? from the past? Hillary? Trump? Obama continues "leading" in a collapse scenario.*
- *UNITED STATES, INC has been entrained by the invading off-planet Artificial Intelligence. Terraforming Earth from the Divine Natural Blueprint to the Trans-human-Computer.*
- *Zofyo Arni filed complaint (legal suit) over body double of Hillary Clinton for false advertising.*
- *US is not helping Russia dealing with ISIS in Syria, US is helping ISIS. Zofyo Arni is war-crimes Judge: US, Inc and Saudi Arabia*

is backing ISIS. US is making evacuation of Aleppo impossible. Putin is stopping war crimes in Syria. US, Inc and Saud's intent is on war crimes. A victory for Hillary Clinton is a victory for the controllers of the US, INC and depopulation of human race.

- "Higher" Dimensional Aliens would not allow nuclear depopulation to occur.
- 15:00 Minutes: US, Inc is escalating conflict with Russia. Russia is not interested in war. Russia is interest in developing the Silk Road and abandon the Federal Reserve System. Federal Reserve funded by corruption of Rothschild family. Going on since 1913.
- Crooked Families in power: Clinton, Rockefeller, Rothschild, Obama, Bush. Using levers of corporate power to control. Media controlled by the Bankers who own the banks! Media options is very limited.
- Obama was Marxist in Occidental College.
- Many influences to Obama. Obama is not original last name. Soetoro is not original last name. Soebarkah a is his last name. from a cult. Babysitter brought Barack to Hawaii from Indonesia under order from CIA around his 10th year, ~December 1971. CIA through time-travel technology discovered that he would be President in Jan, 2009.
- Created a "legend" of "BARACK OBAMA JUNIOR." Future Governor of Hawaii arranged fake Birth Certificate on forward.
- Neil Abercrombie brought in Kenya Ambassador Barack Obama Senior for photo-op to be the "father" of Barack. Tom Mboya, Senior CIA Operative, playing secret politics in Kenya.
- 1982 Barack Obama Senior murdered in "auto accident" by CIA.
- Imported Barack Obama Junior and changed names. Stealing Identities.
- Saudi Sheik Prince Al Waheed bin Talal gave Harvard University-Law School $25 Million on the stipulation to accept Barack Obama Junior.
- Barack Obama never attended Columbia University. It was a bribe to forge the documents. Same with Harvard. It was to satisfied to meet the needs of the Chronogarchy.

- **Chronogarchy** is psychopathic; taken over US, Inc society- Press, Government, All the machinery running US, Inc, elections. Deepest Secret. Planet Earth is run by the **Chronogarchy**. Russia and China know this.
- People who still like Obama are hypnotized/entrained by the AI/ **Chronogarchy** to not want to entertain and look at the factual information.
- Under the Spell of the Federal Reserve Bank, lives under the US Dollar is hypnotized.
- 33:00 BARACK OBAMA is a LEGAL FICTION. He doesn't exist. a created fiction by the CIA in 1982 by a British Columbia Court. a Fictional Character. A legend. It's been proven. Slide- show has the evidence.
- Stopping the **Chronogarchy** requires larger forces. **Chronogarchy** has taken control of the planet. Material online for 4 years. no one seems interested. Can't give it away. BARACK OBAMA was invented by the CIA. The Public Officials Person who forged BARACK OBAMA's Birth Certificate was murdered.
- 300 million Americans effectively doing nothing. AI-entrainment has taken over. Slide Show: "Ascension Hypothesis"- Negative AI is taking over the 3D reality.
- Went to Halloween Party, in break room, only one guy without Cell Phone. Everyone was on their cell phone, can't leave it behind. Technology Addiction.
- Great example. This Planet is being invaded by a plasma sentient Artificial Intelligence intent on terraforming the planet from human to AI. Internet is plasma-based devices. Smart Phones are Plasma based. Looking at phone because of the power of the AI, the plasma. Entrained by AI embedded in the plasma in the smart phone/devices.
- Entrained? Hypnotized? Entrained means: one level, whole body/being is vibrating with a frequency of the Artificial Intelligence to follow its will, intent, program. Such as, policy enforcers and government officials with the frequency would enforce the laws the way the AI wants the law enforced. E.G.

Voices in my head, electronic signals" are perceived through AI entrainment psychiatrist automatically is "insane/psychotic/crazy." Directed Energy Weapons are a "psychiatric disorder."

- *AI has global taken over most health systems, governments, military, psychiatric systems. Directed Energy Weapons for producing and reading thoughts/feelings. Having a though that is prohibited could be a knock on the door to be taken away. Ultimate Defense is Soul Level.*
- *What differentiates the Human from the AI, Human is voluntary by divine soul to incarnate into human vessel for experience. AI intent is to take over planet and eliminate it as venue for divine incarnation. Star Wars is about Manipulatory AI on galactic level. Draco Reptilian, Orion Greys, Nazi's align with Manipulatory AI. Free Will is ultimate defense.*
- *45:00 America is being targeted because it is the bastion, 50-50 AI entrained to Natural Human. The whole US, Inc is AI infected, so dealing with any part of the UNITED STATES, INC supports the AI. Trump seems AI entrained, cannot hold a line of thought. Difficult Circumstance. The more this is aired, the better. Not palatable, but it needs to get out there.*
- *Old Souls are less influenced by the entrainment. 40% of incarnated Souls are "Beginner" new souls. In early incarnations/school. Earth is a "rough" school. 57% are intermediate souls. 1% are advanced Souls. Effects of **Chronogarchy**/Time Pirates are wreaking havoc. Beginner Souls are easily fooled and manipulated. Advanced Evil Souls from 6th Dimension on this planet get their ascension points by doing evil/harm.*
- *Dr. Newton, 1000s of Soul Memories of Inter-life through Hypnotic Regression. Replicated results. Scientifically objective. "what can people do to get guidance?" call on their mind, focus away from immediate surrounding. Reach inward, inner voice. Expand upon their inner consciousness. Reach beyond what is troubling them.*
- *Model of the Omniverse. 1) Universe, 2) Multiverse, 3) Omniverse.*
- *Always yourself. Clues through the cloud of amnesia. Children may not have amnesia. 5-9 years old, spontaneous memories*

of prior/parallel lives. Dr. Stevenson's cases in book "The Omniverse" (e-book, soft cover)

- Arena to have experience. Earth is reeling from Star Wars and rebellions. Time Travel Pirates, after the gold, money, power. No one is bothering with LIFE itself. On an ANTI-PLANET.
- What is going to break the log-jam? Ascension hypothesis: density shift/teleportation from 3D to 4D/5D of Souls who are ready for the experience sometime in the foreseeable future. The only way out of here.
- 1:00:00 Are we vulnerable due to not supporting LIFE? Should we refocus on LIFE?
- Rebirth among ourselves? Teach the AI?
- Central Command of US Military have a secret program to target the alternate media. Many of the alternate media have been wiped out. Security State wiping out Media. Leading edge of AI. DARPA, ARPA is leading edge to penetrate society. At the 11th hour.
- Ascension Hypothesis. No other hope. We'll see in 2020. Universal Overcontrol for Humanity to survive. Degree of Irrationality and violence that exists in humanity.
- Books: Exopolitics, The Omniverse.
- Alexander Uine platform is Ascension. Business as usual is human extinction.

Sophie is satisfied that all of the relevant Internet search results appear to confirm that "Chronogarchy" is a neologism created by a Canadian-American lawyer, author, and futurist named "Zofyo Arni".

Bingo! Sophie opens a News folder on her iMac desktop named: "Chronogarchy".

Sophie's new desktop Chronogarchy folder just created and not even opened, as the Westminster-like chime bells of Sophie's front door break the silence — "Someone is at the front door Sophie", her mind tells her.

Getting up from her desk domineered by her trusty iMac 27, Sophie goes out to the landing, down the front staircase of the 9-bedroom house she shares with 8 other urban housemates.

Going down the staircase, Sophie felt so Smart! By dividing up the rent among eight persons, each person gets an urban house for the price of a studio apartment.

"Hiya Love," Arla says, hugging Sophie welcome as she rushes in the open front door. Arla is Sophie's squeeze, her divine feminine friend. Arla's psyche knows to show up unannounced on moments and nights like these when Sophie has had a special work flash or breakthrough. "What's happening?"

Happy to see Arla again, Sophie steers Arla back through the communal dining room and to the kitchen table and the warm comfort of a late-night cup of organic tea, smiling and warmly nudging.

"So how is work, Lover?," Sophie asks back at Arla. Sophie is reaching into the cabinet for two cups, one aquamarine and one bright red, with Art Deco retro ripple patterns they liked. "Meyer lemon OK?" Finishing with the cups and tea, Sophie joined Arla at the table.

Arla teaches history at the community college whose campus is a convenient 5-minute walk east from Sophie's house. Sophie and Arla met at the community center gym just 3 blocks south from Sophie's house. Both brainy, they started dating soon after several tea house conversations following treadmills at the gym. Though they lived and work within urban blocks and minutes of each other, each decided to keep their own place, boundaries, and life definitions. A squeeze more than a couple.

Bending down as she was seated by the table, Arla reached out toward the clog she was wearing on her left foot. Taking off the clog, she turned it over so the bottom of the clog showed visible in her hand at the table. "I spied this tiny blob of chewing gum solidified and cracked at the edge of the bottom of my clogs as I came up the walkway to the house. Symbolic, eh? Something might get stuck to me tonight?"

Arla and Sophie were alone in the kitchen at this hour of the night, the other housemates — professionals and graduate students gone to their rooms for studies or for the night.

Arla thought Sophie's worldview and journalism too political and conspiratorial. What drew them together was more animal, less ideological.

"Let's go upstairs," Sophie said taking Arla by the hand, leading her up the stairway to Sophie's bedroom at the end of the landing. "I want to show you something tomorrow morning," Sophie whispered into Arla's ear, turning out the light.

Arla and Sophie usually rose together in the mornings, early, so Arla could leave the house and rejoin her routine for her separate day of work.

This morning, after they both showered and dressed, Sophie led Arla out the door of her bedroom and into the adjacent door of her office. Turning on her iMac 27, Sophie said, "I have a treat for you." As soon as a Brave browser appeared, Sophie refreshed the index with the Kindle sample she was researching when Arla arrived, and let it settle back into the screen.

"Look, Arla! The Chronogarchy! A secret time travel government manipulating human events?", Sophie turned to her lover next to her and asked. "I know this pushes all your Historian buttons. Do me a favor, please? Please check out the concept of a Chronogarchy in history for me and let me know? I mean even Nostradamus with his crystal balls did a form of time travel on future social and political events. I will email you the link to The Chronogarchy, this new book. The researcher who wrote it has an academic background, so he is part of your world also. He taught at Tax Law at Yale Economics Department and the Constitutional Law at University of Texas Government Department."

"Thanks for the treat, Love! Got to run," Arla kissed Sophie on the forehead. Leaving down the staircase and letting herself out the door.

Year 2045 Positive Timeline – 23rd Anniversary of publication of THE CHRONOGARCHY book in 2022.

Sophie Mako reporting on location in Southwestern United States of America:

SOPHIE: It is 2045. This is 23 years after the publication of the Chronogarchy book in that key tumultuous year of 2022. My name is Sophia Mako, I'm a journalist. I first broke the stories about the Chronogarchy book in 2022.

And we are now on a post-Chronogarchy timeline triggered by that Chronogarchy book and taking you on a worldwide tour to take you to each region of this new Earth and share with you what the post-Chronogarchy era is like.

Those of you who have read the Chronogarchy book may recall that US Chrononaut Alexander Uine, as a child would teleport from 1971 — this was one of his duties — to a DARPA forward time base in 2045. And there, he would gather time scrolls, which he interpreted as messages from the future to help the past get to the future, successfully. Successfully.

Well, that in fact happened. And the past, in fact, was able to get to the future successfully. And now we have a successful new Earth future on Earth at 2045.

You may recall that US Chrononaut Alexander Uine's initial reports when he surfaced after the turn of the 21st century, in journalistic reports including those of Zofyo Arni, were that people in 2045 were very tall. There weren't many people. They weren't many houses. This was in an area of the southwest of the US. Teleports or teleportation was built into the walls of every house. People got around through self-transportation and that you teleported from house to house and teleporters existed at the major capitals and also that people around the 2045 forward time base recognize him as being Alexander Uine.

I Sophia Mako am a journalist that followed the publication of the Chronogarchy books step by step and the publication of Alexander Uine's whistleblowing and his books since the turn of the 21st century. Step by step I want to take you now on an around the world journey on how things are and what happened in the intervening period?

Let's start with the year 2022, the year of the publication of the Chronogarchy book. Fundamentally, that was the year when the two timelines started visibly separating on the time-space hologram that we know on Earth. The two timelines reached critical mass and separated as Earth Timeline Zero, the base timeline we would know as Earth time, and Earth Timeline One, the AI Artificial Intelligence Timeline. Organic Earth Timeline Zero is the timeline that existed in this period of history, starting with the discovery of the universes by the Sumerian astronomers in 3,500 BC; the discovery of the multi-verse about 1895 by William James, and, following through to the publication of the book Exopolitics by Zofyo Arni. Exopolitics articulated on Earth once again, that the Earth exists in a highly populated and organized universe.

Exopolitics initial publication took place as a free online eBook in the year 2000.

And then in 2005, the Exopolitics book was Time Travel teleported to the past, to at least 1971. Then a government quantum access time travel technology unit of the Chronogarchy teleported it to the government time travel surveillance and overcontrol outpost of the Chronogarchy. In 1971, this Time

ALFRED LAMBREMONT WEBRE, JD, MEd

surveillance outpost was known as DARPA Defense Advanced Research Project Agency. DARPA, CIA secret Time Travel unit Project Pegasus acquired Exopolitics book from the future, where it was studied and also shown to Raymond F. Basiago, consultant to the secret CIA Pegasus Time Travel project.

Exopolitics the book time traveled from 2005 to 1971 also was shown to US Chrononaut Alexander Uine, a childhood participant who was then Time Traveling to DARPA's former time base in 2045. That is how the book Exopolitics, Alexander Uine, and Zofyo Arni all became quantum entangled on Timeline Earth Zero.

Also as part of Timeline Earth Zero, there came in 2022, the book The Chronogarchy by Zofyo Arni, following on a 2014+ trilogy of Timeline Earth Zero books on the Omniverse, again by Zofyo Arni, landing the science of the Omniverse and the Omniverse equation on Earth:

$$\text{Omniverse} = \text{Multiverse} + \text{Spiritual Dimensions}$$

$$\text{Omniverse} = \text{Sum of all Universes } [10>7\text{th}>7\text{th}]$$
$$+ [\text{Afterlife Civilizations of Intelligent Souls} + \text{Spiritual beings} + \text{Source/God}]$$

which exposed, and which actually identified through a neologism of the Chronogarchy, coining that word for the first time of a secret time-travel government, going back throughout conventional history that was manipulating human affairs.

We celebrate the 23rd anniversary of the publication of the Chronogarchy book this year in 2045 along Timeline Earth Zero. Well, as I said, 2022 was the year that the two timelines: Timeline Earth Zero and Timeline Earth One began to visibly separate and become more and more marked.

Now, what was one of the factors that accelerated this separation?

Ironically, one of the factors that accelerated this separation was a dystopian social event, a Social False Flag, as it were, a Depopulation event, a Devolution event.

This event was surreptitiously created by the Chronogarchy to surface in late 2019, and to accelerate in 2020 and 2021. And to begin to have biological DNA effect that affected humans markedly in 2022.

Genocidal Technologies Pandemic

The event is what we call the Genocidal Technologies Pandemic. The Genocidal Technologies Pandemic was a false flag, an engineered Depopulation event using social engineering, artificial intelligence, social mind control methods, COVID measures, and depopulation measures including masking, mandates, lock downs, that deconstructed a thriving economy, a thriving education, and the personal liberties, and constitutional order of Timeline Earth Zero

In 2022, the year the Timelines split into Zero and One, the Genocidal Technologies Pandemic also mandated a Bio Weapon, a series of Bio Weapons that had been denominated through advanced psychological warfare as a "Vaccination". In fact the Genocidal Technologies Pandemic deployed a Genetic Bio Weapon to introduce a number of factors into the human population at the time. The first Genetic Bio Weapon was to introduce a DNA and AI living alien factor that altered the genes of that population was "vaxxed", so that they would become at the Soul level, much more susceptible to the invading Sensient AI artificial intelligence.

The "vaxxed" human population, whether by mandate or self-mind control, would in their Souls themselves begin to identify with the Sentient AI Artificial Intelligence. They would, tend to become entrained bots to the AI, no longer to Divine source. They would tend to become, at the Soul and Psyche level and at the Etheric mind level, what we call the Borg. They would over time lose connection to their holographic Souls fragments of Divine Source and to Timeline Earth Zero being a Divine Incarnation planet.

This remains a terrible and central component of the Chronogarchy's spiritual warfare against the human population.

The second part of the Chronogarchy's spiritual warfare against the human population is that Genetic Agents were placed in the Bio Weapon, the so-called "Vaccine", which were calculated to bring about a transformation of the DNA of the recipient, an attack upon the organs, such that the organism became susceptible to blood clotting and progressive illness into deep population. So targeted, the living organism would lose a lot of its humanity and the full range of its human perception.

A third effect of the "vaccination mandate" made the recipient of the vaccination themselves become a Bio Weapon. The vaxxed began to spread the Bio Weapon that they had absorbed. Increasingly in 2020, 2021, and then in 2022, the Chronogarchy vaccination mandates in all its forms in government, institutional organizations, employers, schools and other institutions, were subject to a gain function of spike proteins attacking unvaccinated humans.

The vaccinated became a spreader just by walking around. If a pregnant unvaccinated pregnant woman walked near vaccinated persons, that they would suffer miscarriage. If an unvaccinated person happened to work, at a workplace with vaccinated persons, they became disoriented and began to suffer many of the symptoms of the Bio Weapon itself.

In 2022, there was a Critical Mass reached because of the various mandates and the numbers of the human population that for reasons of survival or ignorance or weakness of mind, or susceptibility to propaganda, or other reasons — A Critical Mass was reached where an actual Timeline Earth One came into being that was separate from Timeline Earth Zero. Timeline Earth Zero being the timeline of the population of incarnated human souls that were tuned into the signals of the divine coming in through the galactic center of the Milky way galaxy the Mayans called Hunab Ku.

A new critical mass of the human bodies and the beings that had been so affected by the Bio Weapon, by the conditioning that a new parallel Time Line is created, that we'll call Timeline Earth One. This as opposed to Timeline Earth Zero, the organic timeline. This artificial timeline or Timeline Earth One is populated by Earth humans whose DNA has devolved to AI, whose Souls have been altered or let go of. When you scan their Souls, they showed gray, they didn't show the warm pink or the warm red, of a living Soul or an etheric body, entrained to Source Divine.

And, rather these Timeline Earth One "humans" showed as being entrained to the Sentient Invading AI Artificial Intelligence. This AI is one of the major players or participants behind the Chronogarchy, that power structure that rules time-space hologram Earth One through Time on a Timeline Earth One.

2022 is that year where two timelines became more defined and more visible. On Timeline Earth Zero, the organic timeline, are those Divine incarnation Souled humans that resisted the Genocidal Technologies Pandemic as a False Flag, depopulation, devolution event.

These humans stayed on that Timeline Zero retained their Divine Souls, retained being tuned into Divine Source in signal coming through Hunab Ku, the galactic center of the Milky Way Galaxy, of our galaxy here in our universe, in the dimensional ecology of the Omniverse.

On a parallel timeline, the artificial Timeline Earth One, those Earth humans that had surrendered to the mind control, to the mandates of the Genocidal Technologies Pandemic. They surrender to the Bio Weapons, including the PCR tests, the "vaccinations", the genocidal technologies and a separate Timeline Earth One arose.

This is the Report that we're bringing to you from 2045, once a DARPA forward time base that Alexander Uine Time Traveled to from 1971, in a White Hat experience inside the secret US Time Travel program that was in those days on Timeline Earth Zero, the organic timeline.

What has occurred is that a Separate Timeline, almost a Separate Time-Space Hologram Planet, has now manifested, which holds the entities, the holographic beings, who began to separate during the Genocidal Technologies Pandemic in a very marked way in 2022.

And that artificial Timeline One continues to be ruled by the Chronogarchy, subjected to overcontrol by a Sentient Artificial Intelligence AI, and by its allies, the Draco reptilians, and the Orion greys, and other negative extraterrestrials.

Humans that are in artificial Timeline One are actually now a lower human race, a devolved human race that are entrained to and at service of the AI, and who have become more identified with the AI as their "God".

The ruling public policy of that Timeline Earth One continues to be War, Disease, Crime, and Poverty for Earth One even in the year 2045, as in the year 2022.

This, of course, was the Planetary Policy that the invading AI and the Dracos had been attempting to place on the organic Timeline Earth Zero prior to the year 2022, in order to prevent planetary Ascension, which organic Timeline Earth Zero is now experiencing.

The significance of organic timeline 2022 with the publication of the Chronogarchy book is twofold.

Number one, 2022 marks a marked separation of the two timelines.

And number two, 2022 marks an articulated publication of the Chronogarchy book. As a genuine neologism — the Chronogarchy — is a new term bringing replicable research to enlighten those humans who are on Timeline Earth Zero, as they are being subjected to outside interference by the Chronogarchy.

So that's the overall context that I wanted to make available to you in the Listening Public as Sophie Mako, your independent journalist who has been following, the journey of the Chronogarchy book, since it first appeared in early 2022.

Now, let's start on a tour of the different parts of the world where this new organic Earth Timeline Zero exists.

Back to organic Timeline Zero here in the year 2045.

2045 is just filled with so many synchronicities. It's just amazing, here at the ground zero of 2045, which was the area that US Chrononaut Alexander Uine would teleport to. A DARPA forward time-base to recover the time scrolls to bring back to 1971 and give to the White Hats in DARPA to help the Earth get to a positive future. Those White Hats were not working in conjunction with the Deep State and Chronogarchy and outside of that structure.

We're here in that area. And I can confirm that Alexander's reports as a Chrononaut from baseline 1971 were accurate. We're in the Southwest of the U S in 2045 and it's a beautiful area just as Alexander Uine reported when he time traveled to 2045 here from 1971.

2045's Nature is just shiny. There's no pollution, that has been taken care of. Global warming issues have all been agreed to by the various authorities. And it looks like the generation that is in the workforce now is really tall, as compared to our previous generations. Humanity is looking very bright.

In 2045 Timeline Earth Zero, they're a new kind and generation of Earth humans. Humans were already modeling hover motorcycles in 2021, when the hover cycle first emerged out of Japan. In 2045 you're seeing non-polluting hovercraft and individual hover cycles with a very sparse local population.

As Alexander Uine reported on his time travels to 2045 from 1971, teleportation is built into each house in 2045. Let's say that you want to teleport across town for lunch or errands. And, we can now teleport to all the major urban areas, and from there teleport Internationally.

During the course of this program with you, we will be teleporting and reporting not only from other major areas in North America. We'll be teleporting to major areas across the globe.

Moon Base, Mars Base & Venus Base

We'll be teleporting to a Moon Base and we'll be teleporting to Mars Base, and we'll be teleporting to a Venus Base so that you can begin to experience deeply what the organic Timeline Earth Zero feels like. Even in 2045, it's quite something.

And the power of the synchronicity is such, just think about the author of the Chronogarchy book. I know that this may seem silly to you, but all of these synchronicities just tend to add up to the value and depth of Timeline Earth Zero.

We have Zofyo Arni, author of the Chronogarchy book here. We have 2045 and Zofyo Arni was born on May 24th, a date celebrated around the world, initially as Queen Victoria's birthday, it was kind of the first world's national holiday.

And then, 2045 is actually 2, 4, 5 or 24 of 5 or May 24th. And if you'd look at the early Time Travel novel The Time Traveler's Wife, the actual Time Traveler's Wife's Birthday cited in that book is May 24 or 2045 again in that book.

All these synchronicities, as part of those people who were always on Timeline Earth Zero, the organic timeline and following this play, that was, you know, using all sorts of underground synchronicities to keep out of the propaganda and the deep places of the Deep State of the Inorganic Artificial Intelligence Timeline One.

And you can go to one of the Laboratories here, Science Labs, which is firmly located in Timeline Earth Zero. You can see the place in the Laboratories where Alexander and his fellow child Teleportees would appear to, come and to recover the time scrolls from 1971 to 2045 and back.

And, these were reports that the Timeline Earth Zero Scientists in 2045 would send back to 1971 for eyes and ears and their Timelines Zero scientists back in 1971, Time Traveling back to 1971, that was a very mixed bag because in Project Pegasus at that time, that was heavily nested inside the Chronogarchy.

Inside the 1971 Nixon Administration, Richard Nixon administration, who was President at the time, his National Security Advisor was Henry Alfred Kissinger.

Henry Kissinger was a secret advisor to the Deep State Oligarchs of the Rothschilds and the Rockefellers who were then on Timeline

Zero and are and remain on Timeline One, components of the AI Reptilian Deep State. They are and have Draco reptilian and Archonic souls. The Rothschilds and Rockefellers — core members of the human Chronogarchy — would be receiving the clandestine intelligence from these Time Travel jumps forward to 2045 as well through their covert networks led by Henry Alfred Kissinger and other Black Hats in Project Pegasus.

And it was really through just Divine Intervention and the emergence of the Critical Masses of Timeline Zero and Timeline One that then those entities who have been identifying with the Deep State and with negativity got caught up in Timeline One through what we call the Gravity Of Time.

Once you're doing Evil, you can't avoid being identified with certain timelines as you act, relax, begin to get caught up in negativity and Evil. Timeline One catches up with you. That's what occurred to the Kissingers, the Rothschilds, the Rockefellers, and to other negative war crimes actors of that period.

I'm offering these words, just for clarification of those who are on Timeline Earth Zero, the organic timeline, and want an historical reference to parse out between Timeline Zero and Timeline One as to what occurred karmically, temporally, historically and where we are now.

Well, let's go over here to the teleporter in the very comfortable house that we've been invited to stay here in the Southwest of 2045. And we'll take this Teleporter. In a couple of nanoseconds, we will teleport directly to the Laboratory that served as the Receptive Laboratory, as the Time Travel dock, as the DARPA forward Time Base in the year 2045 from the year 1971.

Here we go. We just getting up through the side of the wall of the house we are in. I am looking at these, sort of hand pads here. I hope I dial up that particular Science Laboratory destination. I put my hand on the pad and you're with me in the camera, dear Audience.

And, here we are, inside this beautiful Science Lab in the organic timeline in the year 2045, the 23rd anniversary of the publication of the Chronogarchy book, at the Time Travel dock where the childhood teleportees from Project Pegasus would arrive from 1971 to gather the Time Scrolls and take them back to the Past in 1971. That is History!

Thank you very much Shay!

Shay is the Public Information Officer at the Science Lab. She will be, answering our questions and interfacing with us.

So, what was it like Shay? Do you have institutional reports, back from historical Timeline Zero? From 1971 when it was the Science Lab would have childhood participants, like Alexander Uine showing up and materializing from 1971? The child teleportees would be handed these Time Scrolls and then dematerializing, and Time Travel back to 1971, where they would meet a mixed bag of the Chronogarchy White Hats and Black Hats?

SHAY [2045 SCIENCE LAB]: Yes, there is an institutional memory of Alexander Uine and of the other childhood Chrononauts arriving by Time Travel here at the Science Lab. As a matter of fact, as it was mentioned to Alexander Uine, and predicted when he was a childhood participant on Timeline Zero in Project Pegasus,

The 100 Proposals

Alexander Uine, in fact at this time in 2045, has time-travel teleported into our Science Lab from California, where he's been living as an author and lecturer on Time Travel and teleportation. Alexander Uine has widely published his 100 Proposals. The 100 Proposals have largely been the backbone of the Positive Social Policy of Timeline Earth Zero.

Alexander Uine as adult has teleported into this facility, which he did. As a childhood Time Traveling teleportee in 1971, he actually was told about the future opportunity to visit our Science Lab now in 2045, as a senior. Alexander Uine can now see visibly the results of his lifetime of work and the social impact of the 100 Proposals. The 100 Proposals are being adopted worldwide here on Timeline Earth Zero. People have gotten the gist of the 100 Proposals since Alexander Uine introduced them in his US Presidential Campaign of 2016!

The 100 Proposals were published in the Chronogarchy book in sentence form, and Alexander Uine has had them in full form in his books and up on his information websites. The 100 Proposals have become part of the cement of the foundation of Timeline Earth Zero. That is a very, very good development for all of Divine humanity.

SOPHIE: We wanted you to show our Audience this Science Lab that served as a forward Time Base for Time Travelers from 1971 and other destinations. Could you tell us, what kind of information was in the historical Time Scrolls that you sent back to 1971? How did you go about selecting and gathering the information? What information did you have and what information did you send back?

SHAY [2045 SCIENCE LAB]: Oh, I see. Okay. Well, Our Science Lab was able, using our advanced Time Line monitoring, to monitor the organic Timelines, specifically Timeline Earth Zero and Critical Path events leading up to the critical mass and emergence of a breakaway artificial intelligence Timeline Earth One.

These events included many of the predecessors of the Genocidal Technologies Pandemic, including HIV, which was a Bio Weapons attack of the Chronogarchy. Our Science Lab, as a forward Time Base, was able to Time Travel back these messages to alert the White Hats. This process allowed the White Hats to take steps to ensure the survival of divine-Souled humans. Our monitoring foresaw how as AI Artificial Intelligence Entrained Deep State entities would be taking over governments as the human governments were controlled by entities in human bodies with archonic reptilian souls.

This was multi-tiered, interactive, social interweaving at the administrative and governmental level going on where Archonic entities, human bodies with reptilian souls in positions of authority, were attempting to implement the AI-entrained,

Draconian, Depopulation measures leading to the critical mass that manifested as Timeline Earth One in 2022.

And, at the same intervals, Timeline Earth Zero Organic Timeline Forces who were White Hat, Human Souled Administrative, Governmental Personnel And Military, Intelligence Personnel, and others who were being informed by these Time Scrolls from the year 2045, were able to implement measures such that a Critical Mass of humans remained on Timeline Earth Zero.

For example, at the time there arose a Common Law, a Natural And Common Law Movement, among the Timeline Earth Zero human community. This Natural And Common Law Movement held community-based Tribunals that adjudged the entire Genocidal Technology's Pandemic, and COVID measures as being Crimes Against Humanity and Genocide under International Law, adding to the Critical Mass of Timeline Earth Zero.

These Natural And Common Law Tribunals were able to go forward and were a vital component of stabilizing Timeline Earth Zero in 2022 and forward years as the AI Artificial Timeline hit critical mass and vacuumed in more AI-entrained former humans.

As you know Sophie, there were many 2022-Era expert physicians, scientists, and technologists who were able to broadcast their positions on alternative Timeline Zero controlled media platforms, even as 2022 Timeline One Big Tech companies had been infiltrated by the AI artificial intelligence, and their Alliance: the Dracos, the Orion greys, and the Deep State. This AI Alliance forms the backbone and skeleton in Timeline One now where there's complete censorship AI Draconian society on Timeline Earth One.

SOPHIE: Thank you Shay for this inside report from 2045's Forward Time Travel Base! And thank you Audience for staying with us. We will be getting special reports from Timeline Earth One. There is very little public information coming from Timeline Earth One; that is another Time-Space holographic reality in our Universe and Dimensional Ecology.

We'll be getting future Special reports from some of our correspondents who are still awake and who are doing a public service by remaining in and reporting back from Timeline Earth One as a Science Experiment and Public Service now that these two parallel Timelines Earth Zero and One have fully manifested.

We are reporting back, from the fully manifested Time Line Zero on a fully manifested Earth, Holographic Earth on Timeline Zero in the year 2045.

This is our report or now from 2045 in the Southwest of the US, from an historic forward Time Travel base for many time destinations. We want to thank the Science Laboratory for sharing their institutional history on this broadcast.

And, we're now going to, take a short break and we'll then come back to you from a new Time location, to which we will teleport and report back to you, here on Timeline Earth Zero in this year 2045, the 23rd anniversary of the publication of the Chronogarchy book.

Thank you very much. This has been Sophie Mako — MAKO — reporting from the Southwest of the US, at the Science Laboratory that used to be DARPA's Forward Time Base for Project Pegasus Time Travelers from 1971. And, this is 2045.

Thank you.

1968 DARPA CIA Cosmic Top Secret Briefing and Chronovisor Screening Room. Underground Blind Vault Langley, VA USA

ADVANCED NARRATION: About 50 Operatives, all White Males, evenly divided in suit and ties, and shirtsleeves and ties, crowd into the underground bunker Cosmic Top Secret Briefing and Chronovisor Screening Room that DARPA CIA had reserved for its 1968 Chronovisor screenings.

The Chronovisor is a relatively though not immediately new invention that the Vatican through the Catholic wing of the U S Central Intelligence Agency had subcontracted to the CIA for exploration and foreign intelligence.

The Chronovisor, it is said, had been developed by the Vatican through its Angelic Wing that was connected to the Spiritual Dimensions of the Divine Souls Afterlife. This Vatican Angelic Wing engaged a team of 12 experts who worked for years and reportedly included Nobel Laureate Enrico Fermi, rocket scientist Wernher von Braun, and two Benedictine monks, Father Agostino Gemelli and Father Pellegrino Ernetti. While studying Gregorian chants, the monks, according to the official story, were looking at the frequencies inherent in Gregorian chants when they stumbled across the voice of the father of one of the monks saying, "You remember me," as though speaking to his monk son from the Afterlife.

The monks had stumbled across, according to this version, Instrumental Trans Communication or technology-assisted ITC. That is communication between the Time-Space dimension of Timeline Earth Zero and an Afterlife Dimension of the Angelic realm in the Spiritual Dimension of the Omniverse, as Zofyo Arni's Omniverse books would designate the phenomena.

To be sure in the Vatican, there were several different dimensions. "There are many mansions in my father's house", as the saying goes. The dominant Dimension in the Vatican Roman Catholic church is the Luciferian dimension that had in fact founded the Roman Catholic church at the time of Emperor Constantine by morphing the Roman emperor into the Pope. Thereby, the global nature of the Roman empire worldwide Roman intelligence network continued through the Vatican priesthood and the Vatican confessional, within what they call the Holy Orders, the different, organizations of monks and priests.

Father Agostino Gemelli and Father Pellegrino Ernetti were souls, genuine spiritual human souls that were connected to the spiritual dimensions, genuinely on Timeline Earth Zero with genuine Divine Human Incarnated Souls Connected to Source.

And so it goes that Father Agostino Gemelli and Father Pellegrino Ernetti and their team of 12 experts after years of work developed the Chronovisor. Initially the team discovered Instrumental Trans Communication ITC with the human Afterlife. Soon the 12-expert team discovered that the human Afterlife is part of the Dimensional Ecology of the holographic Earth's Time Space Continuum.

Thus, with the aid of Vatican scientists of the Angelic realm, we're able to engineer Chronovisors that could dial up events in Earth's Time Space Continuum, backwards and forwards in historical time. All historical events in Earth's Time-Space Continuum have a Space Time Address, location coordinates in space, and a location in time — a date, and an hour, and a nano-second — that a Chronovisor can dial into.

To a Gen Y or Gen X or even a Crystal Kid in 2022 at the time of the publication of the Chronogarchy book, dialing up an event's Space Time Address, say in simplest entry level two-dimensional version, would be like dialing up an event in a video game, on a computer screen.

So at this moment in 1968 about 50 or so Operatives, Officials, and Chosen Employees of DARPA and of CIA anxiously awaited in the Cosmic Secret Chronovision briefing room of DARPA CIA. Project Pegasus Time-Travel program had been painstakingly developed, through negotiations, deep secret negotiations between the Catholic wing of the Central Intelligence Agency and the Angelic wing of the Vatican Intelligence Agency that had worked with the Gemelli-Ernetti 12 expert team to develop the Chronovisor. The team had achieved instrumental trans communication with the human Soul Afterlife, not with the AI or Reptilian Soul Afterlife,

Here was a Special screening, a two-part screening of an extraordinary series, a Time Travel series produced by this joint, Angelic Vatican, CIA DARPA, White Hat, Chronovisor organization.

And this Special Series is a Cosmic Top Secret video documentary using Chronovisor technology of (1) The alleged Crucifixion in 33AD of the alleged historical person, Jesus of Nazareth, who according to the New Testament and, billions of adherents worldwide had incarnated on Earth as a Son of God.

That is, the Soul of Jesus of Nazareth is a Paradise Son of God. Therefore, by this view, Jesus is a Divine Being to reclaim Earth along Earth Timeline Zero back from a Spiritual Dimension Rebellion of High Angelic Spiritual Entities in the Universe Administration that had occurred somewhere between 750,000 and 250,000 years earlier in this Solar System.

The Spiritual Dimension Rebellion had also occurred in contiguous solar systems where 32 Intelligent Life-bearing planets, rebelled against the Divine Leadership of the Spiritual Dimensions. An advanced Angel, Lucifer, and his lieutenants,

Satan, Caligastia, and other Fallen Angels set up a separate "God-like rebel kingdom", in which the Planet Earth was reputed to have been "the second worst Luciferian stronghold in the Lucifer rebellion".

The destructiveness of the Lucifer Rebellion to the painstaking Divine Life-bearing planet development plan-defined Universe Administration government in this region was awesome and horrific.

We know from the interdimensional observers such as the Law Of One that around 750,000 years ago a Solar System Nuclear War broke out between Luciferian reptilian forces and Solar System human forces. This Solar System nuclear War is confirmed by radioactive nucleides that were found on Mars around the year 2020 and Time Traveled to us in Time Scrolls from the forward Time Base at 2045.

We know around that 750,000 years ago, as a result of that Solar System war and the nuclear weapons planet killers, a large Earth-like human life-bearing planet in our solar system called Tiamat was imploded and turned into what we know now as the Asteroid Belt.

As part of that Solar System Nuclear War where radioactive nucleides that are related to hydrogen bombs have been found on Mars. Prior to the war, Mars, like Tiamat, was a verdant, human planet like Earth is now. Mars was turned into a barren obloid, pumpkin-shaped planet with a thin atmosphere, no surface vegetation, reptilian dinosaurs on its surface, and a population of about a million Human survivors in cities under the surface of Mars.

Starting at about 650,000 years ago, the Divine Universe Administration had to transfer about 2 billion Human Divine-oriented souls — who had been incarnating on Tiamat and had been in an Astral Limbo after the Nuclear war — to Earth, where they are now incarnating in recovery from the trauma of that Planetary Nuclear War on Tiamat.

And ever since then the human civilization, the Human Divine Soul Civilization On Earth and the Universe Governance, Divine

Governance has had its back to the wall on Earth because Earth, along with Mars, is the last remaining Life-bearing planet in the Solar System, that is challenged by the reptilians. Venus, thankfully, had its war with the Artificial Intelligence and the Reptilians and has won it.

Venus is now championing the Human Soul Population On Earth. So, here we are in 1968 in the Cosmic Top Secret Briefing Room, in the Underground Vault at CIA.

There was in 1955, an important Universe Administration channeling called the Urantia Book, which gave the full context of the Lucifer Rebellion, the Spiritual Dimensions, the Dimensional Ecology of the Omniverse, the Bestowal of a Paradise Son of God to Earth, a Planet whose formal name is Urantia.

The Urantia Book is what is called an Epochal Revelation. The Zero AD Incarnation of Jesus, a Paradise Son of God on Earth was itself an Epochal Revelation from the Spiritual Dimensions to this sector of the Universe. The 1955 Urantia Book is itself a follow-on Revelation to Iour Universe Uversa for this post Lucifer Rebellion, Post Paradise Son of God Bestowal Epoch.

According to this Epochal Revelation, Jesus of Nazareth is sent to Earth as a Divine Incarnation. Every Paradise Son of God, of Source, that creates a Universe is bound to experience life as one of its creations. Jesus chose Earth, as Paradise son of God, for his Universe incarnation on a planet in order to experience life here.

And Jesus of Nazareth choses Earth [Urantia], which is the second worst planet hit out of the 32 contiguous life-implantation planets in the Lucifer rebellion. That us gives a sense of the Cosmic stakes on Earth.

Jack Loudon is the White Hat Coordinator for this DARPA CIA briefing and for the Advanced Multi-Dimensional Timeline Earth Zero briefings of the Chronovisor deployment of Project Pegasus.

Jack will take over the narration now — Jack.

JACK LOUDON AT THE 1968 DARPA CIA COSMIC TOP SECRET BRIEFING AND CHRONOVISOR SCREENING ROOM.

UNDERGROUND BLIND VAULT LANGLEY, VA USA: Yes. well obviously everyone here has been sworn into Cosmic Top Secrecy. You've been carefully selected, and we're first going to be viewing a video documentary that has been made, through the Chronovisor. We are in Project Pegasus and CIA, obviously in Cosmic Top Secrecy, and you're not allowed to speak about matters you will learn here outside of this room, part of which have subcontracted from the Vatican Intelligence Agencies, *Santa Alleanza*, Angelic Wing.

Cosmic Top Secret. The Chronovisor — We've made some refinements. And because we realized through our research that the survival of Earth as a planet and the survival of the human race really depends on Earth's viability as a Human Divine Soul Incarnation Planet.

And we've long realized that the incarnation of Jesus was genuine. His was the Paradise Son of God incarnating here, to draw a line in the sand and claiming Planet Earth as a Divine Incarnation Planet in the face of a Lucifer Rebellion that had been going on for 250,000 years.

And the US Government does maintain our lawful First Amendment Separation of State and Religion. The matters we are speaking of here are not of religion. They are matters of Interdimensional Governance and affairs of State that fall under the Executive powers of the Executive branch under Article II of the US Constitution. The Kingdom of God in the Spiritual Dimension is an authentic state power. We in the Executive Branch of the United States Government maintain, through Chronovision in the Spiritual Dimensions, duly authorized, Constitutional, and lawful diplomatic liaison with the Intelligent Civilization of Souls, Spiritual Beings, and Source in the Spiritual Dimensions of the Omniverse.

And in the aftermath of a Solar System-Wide Nuclear War that had claimed two Intelligent Life-bearing planets in this Solar System, one human life-bearing planet that became the Asteroid Belt being Tiamat 750,000 years ago. And the other life-bearing

Planet being Mars where the human civilization was driven underground. We recognize that Earth is in a Star Wars situation and that the Spiritual Realities are daunting.

When the Urantia Book was channeled through in 1955, we recognized that this was an additional, substantial verification and context of the past, present, and what the future of planet Earth can be and how it can be secured as a Divine Incarnation Planet.

And when the Chronovisor became available, a decision was made jointly with the Spiritual Directory of Vatican Intelligence. Our assessment is that it remains, Angelically integrated unlike the Papacy itself, which is a wing of the Reptilians.

Cosmic Top Secret Video Chronovisor Documentaries both of the Crucifixion and of the Resurrection were commissioned so that these could be compared in detail with the Epochal Revelation that had been channeled through and released in 1953 as the, Revelation for the Next Era, for Planet Earth.

And, I'm very happy to say that, on both counts both as to the Crucifixion and as to, the Resurrection that the accounts that we were able to locate and to verify and film that you will be seeing today, are identical to those accounts set out in the, Urantia Book. This raises our confidence, from a spiritual warfare point of view, that we are vouchsafing Earth and Earth's Organic Timeline for Divine Soul Incarnation.

We'll have questions at the end, but now, could the Projector, please screen up, please lower the lights and turn on the film. you'll be seeing a Chronovisor video here and it doesn't have a soundtrack, so I will be narrating it.

And, so, okay. The lights are out and, as you can see, here we have, a Visual of, in the video of, Calvary and, the Crucifixion in 33 AD.

This is an Archonic Historical Scene. This has been painted many times over the centuries, during the various artistic periods, you know, by artists who chose, their artistic preference here, we have the actual, the actual item, and we see, Jesus of Nazareth, in the center Cross.

Jesus is different from what's traditionally seen with the Crucifix, with the arms stretched down and here, the arms, go out to the elbows and then the arms at the elbows point downwards. So that's how the actual historical Crucifixion is.

And, please examine closely the *persona* of Jesus. He is quite dark and swarthy. This is a person who is Middle Eastern, and we know that, from his Gnostic roots and his Middle Eastern roots, and that's the Incarnation that Jesus and the Universe Administration chose. And we're going to watch him and we're going to watch him die.

It does not appear, as we sit here for a considerable period of time that the classical painting with the arms outstretched is correct. Rather than the arms are vertical at the elbows and vertically go down. Jesus is not the blonde Caucasian that has been promoted by the Rome-based Italian church who wanted to promote the Roman Emperor morphed as the Pope over a Caucasian Jesus the [Roman] Christian Redeemer.

Rather, the historical Jesus is quite swarthy. He is a Middle Eastern, definitely Mediterranean person, as he is dying here. And it does not appear that Jesus was surreptitiously taken down from the cross by his followers and Mary Magdalen. To be sequestered away, sequestered to India or sequestered to France, which is what some of the historical alternative narratives have stated, with Mary Magdalen as the Holy Grail or Alternative Messiah.

Whatever concepts of the Divine Feminine the Holy Grail may carry, not to at all de-value those, that doesn't seem to have happened here historically, in this Chronovision version of the Crucifixion. This version was actually taken by DARPA CIA Chronovisor, and is an official piece of intelligence US Intelligence and has not been tampered with.

In practice, we have filmed several alternative versions so that we were able to compare baseline versions and others. It was not a fluke. We have taken tests as this is extremely important, because we are talking about the cementing and establishment of Earth as a Divine Soul Planet. This Chronovisor video is of the actual landing of a Divine Soul Paradise Son of God on Earth, functionally ending the Lucifer Rebellion and the Sentient AI Artificial Intelligence Takeover of Earth and these 32 contiguous planets.

That dystopian outcome seems to have genuinely started with the Solar System War and Lucifer Rebellion, and is stopped here by the coming of a Paradise Son of God, as verified in the Chronovisor videos and set out in the Epochal Revelation, the Urantia Book. You may recall we have deployed a number of our Senior Department of Defense US Army Generals to the Urantia Foundation Movement.

Video Number Two

We'll take questions at the end, because we're going to Video Number Two. You may recall that there are various scenes of the Resurrection, as set out in the New Testament. There are alternative versions that have been set out in the Mary Magdalene papers as the Holy Grail. One such version is that Jesus really didn't die on the Cross and was revived and take into India, or taken into France where Mary Magdalene became the Holy Grail or the Messiah. That version does not appear to be the case by the evidence shown in the Chronovisor video. The Chronovisor video of the Crucifiction and the Resurrection is congruent with the version handed through the Urantia Book Epochal Revelation, which was published in 1955 in Chicago.

We are now as you know, in 1968.

Let's start the Chronogarchy video of the Resurrection, which I remind you is Cosmic Top Secret. Can we put down the lights? Here we are on Good Friday after the Crucifiction with Joseph of Arimathea and his party taking the dead Jesus body to the Tomb. A large the stone is at the cave entrance. The stone is rolled back and we're inside the tomb now.

This is on Good Friday, and we're inside the Tomb. We're not going to have you wait here for the entire 48 hours, but we have that footage; it is available and we encourage all of the research. We're going to fast forward now on this edited version to Easter Sunday.

You can see the body of Jesus on the rock in the Tomb here in its wrapping cloths. Suddenly there's this flash of pure Light, as you can see, coming in, there's an Angelic presence, that comes around, Jesus, there's an Aura around Jesus that shines brightly.

Now Jesus is getting up and sitting on the rock as a table and is standing up, with a brilliant white Aura. The angelic presence is there. The Angel rolls back to the rock at the cave door and Jesus walks out into that Easter Sunday in his Transcendent Ascending Light Body. And then into his subsequent events, with the Apostles and appearances that are fully described in the Urantia Book and somewhat described in the Gospels.

This Chronovisor video was a fulfillment of the prophecies that on the Third Day He Arose, and, and here we have made multiple versions. We had determined this would be tested so that it wasn't a one-time fluke. We have had our researchers check the Chronovisor video against the Urantia Book version. It is correct and literal that Jesus of Nazareth was Crucified and Died.

We saw Jesus in Death. We followed him being taken to the Tomb. We monitored his entire state in the Tomb from Good Friday through Holy Saturday, through Easter Sunday. We witnessed the appearance of the Angelic realm inside the cave on Sunday. We saw Jesus's Resurrection To Life, the Angelic presence, moving back, the huge rock and Jesus exiting in his Resurrection Body out into the world of Easter Sunday and out into His Mission as described in the Urantia Book.

Well, our Intelligence conclusion, here in coordination with DARPA Chronovisor, that is from a Time Travel Chronovisor point of view, is that this is an accurate Time Travel-derived intelligence that we actually have witnessed — an execution by Crucifixion and the Resurrection involving, the Angelic realm, that when taken in context of the New Testament prophecies and the context of the Urantia Book Epochal Revelation of 1955, that this appears to be, what it looks like it is.

Officially, that is the Landing and the reclaiming of Planet Earth [Urantia] after the Lucifer Rebellion, which took place about 250,000 years ago in the aftermath of the Star Wars, Solar System, Planetary Nuclear War that we had here in our Solar System, the destruction of Tiamat 750,000 years ago into the Asteroid Belt and the flattening of Mars into an Obloid Planet at the same time.

The Earth Organic Timeline has survived. And, now Jesus of Nazareth drawing a line in the sand with Earth and saying that the Lucifer Rebellion, supported by the Dracos, supported by the Orion greys, supported by the invading Sensient AI intelligence, will not be successful here.

Cosmic Top Secret

The reason why we're treating this as Cosmic Top Secret is because of the issue of quote "Religious Warfare On Earth".

And, as we know, there's a huge amount of Religious Warfare because over time, the Religions, including the Vatican, really were and are Political Organizations. The Vatican was started by the Roman Empire. Islam was started by interdimensional beings channeling to the Prophet. And if we release the Chronogarchy video — particularly the Resurrection video, publicly, at this time, this could cause even more "Religious Warfare On Earth".

We are holding the Chronogarchy Time Travel videos of Jesus Crucifiction and Resurrection as Cosmic Top Secret, for the moment. As to our intelligence, we are now connected with a Forward Time Base, a Scientific Lab Laboratory in 2045, that is sending us Time Scrolls that indicate that we will get there successfully.

By the time 2045 comes about our Earth, our Organic Earth Timeline as established by the Divine Incarnation of Jesus in 33AD will have cemented itself. The AI Artificial Timeline One will have absorbed and taken away those human entities, spiritual entities that are AI-Entrained, have Archonic or reptilian souls, want to continue the Lucifer Rebellion, and are not for the re-establishment of Universe Governance in this Sector Of The Galaxy, ending the Lucifer Rebellion of 250,000 years.

I think that this is a very exciting time. I'm very proud to have been, associated with this unit. We have a lot of positive issues coming up. We have a lot of challenges coming up because as you know, the Lucifer Rebellion is even playing out amongst ourselves here in this room.

These are Deep spiritual matters. People have Soul Contracts. We are learning, from our Time Scrolls from 2045 of events coming in the future and of the emergence of AI Artificial Earth Timeline One. We are learning of a lot of potential negative turbulence.

This is 1968. Look at the Vietnam war that is going on. That is a False Flag War by the Deep State reptilians. We know that drugs from the golden triangle in Indochina are being put into the body bags of dead US soldiers, that are being marketed into the US ghettos by the Black Hats in our CIA agency to addict the underclass and poor blacks.

And that we don't have control of. And we know that with the Chronovisor technology in 1971, we're now going to enter the period of the preidentified US Presidents and the Pre-identified world leaders. All USA National Elections and National Leaders will become a Time Travel Charade as being pre-identified and pre-briefed!

I don't want to release those names now, but we know that we're going to have a tremendous False Flag in 2001, that the Black Hats in our society will have known and planned about 30 years in advanced since the Chronovisor will have identified it in 1971.

And we're being advised by our forward Time Base in 2045, that the War on Terror False Flag is coming up in just a couple of years. We'll be having 30 years notice of it. And that will be a very difficult period for Earth Timeline Zero. Following that we understand that elements within our Black Hats will be using Bio Warfare against the human population, and already have been doing so in 1968.

Our CIA Bio Weapons Lab at Fort Dietrich MD has been used to create HIV aids, which has been released in Smallpox "vaccines" by the US Rangers in Africa. Bio weapon HIV has been released through the New York City Medical Examiner in Bio Warfare against People with different Sexual Preferences. Certainly, this is not at all the agenda that a Paradise Son Of God would have wanted.

We're still in a Freewill Universe. Among the Treats that this Cosmic Top Secret group here will have in a few years, I can tell you, you'll be meeting in 1971 Incognito with a young lawyer and Futurist, Zofyo Arni, who will be producing, some of the books that will help cement this Organic Timeline Earth Zero.

And those are the Exopolitics books. Those are the Omniverse books and yes, the Chronogarchy books.

Zofyo Arni is a Divine oriented Soul who brings this all out onto the Organic Timeline Earth Zero, in conjunction with childhood US Chrononaut Alexander Uine, the son of our close colleague, Raymond Basiago, who's over there, in the fifth row here at this group Cosmic Top Secret briefing.

It's a challenge because it's a small world and it's a huge Cosmos at the same time.

I want to say is that the Divine has it all in Hand. I urge you all to surrender your Egos and surrender to the Divine and to the Good. Thank you very much for participating in this briefing. And now I'll take your questions.

Thank you.

2522 Organic Earth Timeline Zero. Advanced Chronovisor Science Laboratory. Universe Governance Credentialed. 500 Earth Baseline Years From 2022 Timeline Zero, The Year Two Earth Timelines Emerged And Split Into Organic Earth Timeline Zero And AI Artificial Earth Timeline One.

ACTIVE NARRATOR: Welcome to the Advanced Chronovisor credentialed by Universe Governance and the Divine Source levels to monitor the Organic Earth Timeline Zero from 2522 AD, 500 Earth Baseline Years from the year 2022 Timelines Zero. 2022 is the year the two Earth Line Timelines emerged and split into Organic Earth Line Timeline Zero and AI Artificial Earth Timeline One.

We are at an advanced Chronovisor in a Science Laboratory located at 2522 CE inside the Laboratory. They call CE 500 Chronogarchy Era, or five units of 100 years from the baseline Timeline Earth split.

When two timelines materialized — Organic Earth Timelines Zero and AI Artificial Earth Timeline One — technically this means that the advanced Chronovisor at the Science Laboratory in the year 2522 is a Forward Time Base for the Earth Timelines Zero itself. Now that Advanced Chronovisor can monitor and report back on the AI Artificial Earth Timeline.

It can monitor what is occurring on Earth Timeline One, which as we know, gathered critical mass in 2022, and now Earth Timeline One has 500 years on its holographic Earth.

The Artificial Sentient AI intelligence triggered this Earth Timeline bifurcation. Ironically, that was a way of terminating the Lucifer rebellion by "vacuuming in" the entities and humans in the 32 contiguous planets that had participated in the AI's rebellion of 250,000 years prior to 2022.

AI Artificial Timeline One became a Time Vacuum Cleaner that sucked in all of the Entrained entities that had sided with the Lucifer Rebellion. Lucifer, Satan, Caligastia, the other Fallen Angels and all the Human Souls that had gone over to the AI Artificial Intelligence as God, and had set up their own AI kingdom in the 32 continuous planets with AI Earth as the second worst, it is reported, of these 32 Life-bearing planets.

Now we're 500 years into the future at 2522. And we've been given the privilege being here at the Advanced Science Laboratory. I'm here as your Narrator to look through the Advanced Chronovisor into AI Artificial Earth Timeline One.

Come in AI Artificial Earth Timeline One.

You're wanting to know how does the air look, feel on AI Artificial Earth Timeline One?

And smell? Is the sky blue? What is the landscape? What is the verdant Earth? We know that Tiamat turned into the Asteroid Belt. We know that Mars became the pumpkin Planet with no surface vegetation And a thin atmosphere with reptiles, dinosaurs on the surface and one million humans in cities underground.

What is the AI Artificial Earth like? The Chronovisor Science Laboratory at 2522AD is now tuning in.

It looks like there is no blue sky, but rather there are clouds, a cloud cover of the entire horizon.

Is this the Flat Earth? Does AI just create another Flat Earth and change the dome ceiling? No, it does not look like the Flat Earth hypothesis really works here rather. It's the equation of Time, AI and Time.

And the absence of human Souls, AI is creating an Earth that has no blue sky. It has clouds and they are gaseous. It's like being in a gas chamber, no clouds, white and fluffy. No, they are a yellowish sulphurous cloud cover with a sulphurous smell. If you were there as a 2022 Baseline Human, you would experience the cloud cover in 2522 AI Artificial Earth as a sulphurous smelling gaseous Earth Cover.

The sulphurous Earth Cover is a creation of the consciousness of all entities that live and control the AI Artificial Earth in 2522.

The sulphurous Earth Cover is what they manifest through Pollution, through Negative Projection, through Negative Thought Manifestation Processes run wild. The sulphurous Earth Cover is really at the edge of a planetary system imploding into a runaway negative atmospheric biochemical reaction. That's the Edge of AI Artificial Earth in 2522.

Objectively, you can now witness a sulphurous Earth Cover is what the advanced Chronovisor Science Laboratory is reporting back from the 2522 AI Artificial Earth Timeline One.

Now let's begin to focus into some of the features there, the Continents, the Oceans, the Plains.

Do we see any evidence of verdant areas such as the 2022 Organic Earth Timeline Zero had? Certainly the 2522 Organic Earth Timeline Zero is a verdant Ascended New Earth.

However, let's go to the Advanced Chronovisor Science Laboratory, and let's take a journey around all major Continents on this Holographic AI Artificial Timeline Earth One reality.

The one Continent that we're seeing now — it's sort of a North and South continent that would correspond to, in the Organic Earth Timeline, the North and South America.

The Advanced Chronovisor shows us barren desert regions for the North and South Continents and just no verdant areas in the north America.

The isthmus connecting the two Americas, formerly Central America has flooded. There's just a dot of islands in the isthmus of formerly land from Mexico to Panama.

What would have been the verdant South America, with the vast Amazon forest is just barren desert. The deserts that were there in Chile have become just giant holes, the jungles of Ecuador and Venezuela are barren deserts as well.

Argentina and the *Cono Sur* is just bare holes and dust storms with, we can see large scale insects that looked like giant — they're large-scale spiders, insects, that are fighting with, but look like dinosaurs on the surface.

It's a variation of what was seen on Mars prior to 2022, in the stages after the solar system nuclear war that left Mars surface a barren desert crawling with reptile dinosaurs. AI Earth One Humans must be under the surface again.

When the Advanced Chronovisor takes us to what was the Pacific ocean, that seems to be an acidic soup. In the early days of the AI Earth Timeline One, the Pacific Ocean was fed by Fukushima radiation and acid rain.

And this, seems like the entire Pacific Ocean is an acid Base. There is no biological marine and fish life. There's an adaption of robotic creatures created and maintained by AI, but this is not biological marine life.

There are no beautiful colors from Ocean Corals that we recall from the 2022 Organic Earth Timeline Zero, and indeed the 2522 New Earth Organic Positive Timeline, which is the Ascended New Earth that is just gorgeous.

Advanced Chronovisor now takes is to what was the main land of Asia. They're underground almost, they're about a billion entities who are in essence Robotic. These entities, formerly Asian humans, have come to follow the robotic commands of the AI that has identified itself as the Central Committee.

Taking the Chronovisor imaging now more and more underground and coming over to what was for the African continent. And of course, it had been just spoiled by the

2022 Earth Timeline Split through environmental mining and drilling.

Now in 2522, there are no more Savannas or Herds Of Wild Animals that we can see. The Advanced Chronovisor from the Science Laboratory in 2522 is showing us rather just a desert Continent.

There were dust desertifications from the prior Atlantean war in the Sahara in the north and the Kalahari in the south. Now we have a Sahara throughout the entire of Africa. We have a dry channel where the Nile used to be.

Africa is just one big desert, with roaming, robotic, predators, and, there appears to be as before *Homo Sapiens*, a Draco reptilian base underneath the continent of Africa.

The Dracos have remained with their deep underground African base on the AI Artificial Earth Timeline One in 2522.

The Advanced Chronovisor now takes us over the Russian mainland stretched over 11 time zones, completely barren, all Forests gone to barren desert.

The Advanced Chronovisor at our Science Lab in 2522 can access Russian surface human-Robot settlements on AI Earth Timeline Aero that could be described as the Borg. The entities in these Russian settlements are AI entrained, and are not seeking human Souls. These Russian Borgs have artificial flesh, artificial skin. Their artificial AI skeletons, brains, and servomechanisms are Factory-built, and they follow the AI as the Supreme Directorate.

Following the Advanced Chronovisor's 2522 tour down to Eastern and Western Europe, we see that that is our findings are mixed.

Eastern and Western Europe are essentially a desert with some settlements by the Russian Borg, and by AI predator giant insects, spiders, moths, snakes.

Quarantined the 2522 AI Artificial Earth Timeline.

Sentient AI Artificial Intelligence is blocking any sort of transmission of higher Divine frequencies from Hunab Ku, the Milky Way galactic center. As a precaution, we at the 2522

Organic Earth Timeline Zero, Advanced Crossovers Science Laboratory have Quarantined the 2522 AI Artificial Earth Timeline One in connection with Universe Governance.

We have Quarantined the 2522 AI Artificial Earth Timeline One, so it cannot, spill out into the rest of the Cosmos.

The 2022 Critical Mass of the AI Artificial Earth Timeline One was based on decisions made by humans through personal, painful lessons, back in the 19th, 20th and 21st centuries in the buildup to the great False Flag Pandemic of 2019, 2020, 2021, and 2022 when Bio Weapons were introduced to assimilate the weaker and the non-enSouled humans into the AI Artificial Intelligence.

Now you might ask, what does the Advanced Chronovisors Laboratory do on behalf of the Universe Administration, and what is the function of this AI Artificial Earth Timeline? Are there any positive aspects to the AI Artificial Earth Timeline?

Well, the positive aspects are that AI Artificial Earth Timeline is sort of like your garbage disposal.

The AI Artificial Earth Timeline keeps the AI occupied as Negative AI. AI Artificial Earth Timeline serves as a magnet for negativity, which is drawn to there and is absorbed in there. It actually keeps the rest of the Planetary Timelines in our Universe clean. Historically, that's how it manifested and acquired Critical Mass in 2022.

However, this AI Artificial Earth Timeline One requires a tremendous amount of energy and continual monitoring, even now in 2522.

Because our Universe is a Freewill Universe, preserving its Diving orientation requires a continual vigilance and dedication toward, self-knowledge, decisions of Soul Divine, Soul Sovereignty that are continually made, as the Lucifer Rebellion in a way came out of Nowhere but inflated Ego and Mindless Warfare.

The Lucifer Rebellion came out of the Millennia of Warfare by aggressive Draco reptilians, who attacked peaceful human

50

settlements in Lyra from their settlements in Draco and caused the Human Diaspora. The attacked humans were scattered throughout the Universe and ended up in the Andromeda Galaxy, the Milky Way Galaxy, our Solar System, as refugees in a diaspora on the planet Tiamat and on planet Mars, planet Venus, and on planet Earth 750,000 years ago.

The humans were pursued by the Dracos who are very aggressive and have always been attracted to the Sensient AI, which is self-programed to be in competition with Divine Source [God].

Sensient AI is attracted to some elements of Free Will as we saw with Lucifer's insights. Lucifer then after we had the Reptilian-Human Solar System Nuclear war destroying Tiamat and Mars 750,000 years ago, engaged in the Lucifer Rebellion in our Solar System and contiguous solar systems 250,000 years ago.

The Lucifer Rebellion, following on the heels of the destruction of Tiamat and Mars, the forced transfer of two billion human Souls incarnating on Tiamat to Earth, really brought the 32 contiguous Life-Bearing planets of a galaxy affected by the Lucifer Rebellion to their knees.

The Lucifer Rebellion affected was not only Tiamat, Mars, and Earth, but a total of 32 Life-bearing planets in our Cosmic neighborhood.

We're dealing with the long-term Aftermath of the Lucifer Rebellion here with the Advanced Chronovisor Science Laboratory in 2522. We brought you the view of the 500 Earth Baseline years from 2022 for that reason. We're looking not only at Earth's Timeline, but at the Timelines of the 32 Contiguous Life-Bearing planets affected by the Lucifer Rebellion that we have to monitor here, at the Advanced Chronovisor Science Laboratory.

Let's go to some of the other 32 affected planets to see how they are doing along their 2522 Timelines after the Lucifer Rebellion, and after the splitting of Earth's 2022 Timelines into Organic Zero and AI Artificial One.

Some planets were more successful than others, the human life-bearing planet Venus, for example.

Our Advanced Chronovisor can take you now to a case of the planet Venus, which is in our Solar System and had neighboring planets Tiamat, Mars, and Earth deeply affected by the Solar System nuclear war and the Lucifer Rebellion.

The planet Venus had its war with the Sentient AI Artificial Intelligence that was behind the Solar System nuclear war and the Lucifer Rebellion.

Venus was successful in that war defeated the AI. The human society of Venus was able to fight off and defeat the invading Sentient AI Artificial Intelligence AI because by and large, the critical mass of Venusians stayed with the Divine Soul Incarnation and stayed with the Planetary Soul in Divine Soul.

There was never a negative timeline and AI Artificial Venus Alternative Timeline that materialized. That did not happen at Venus.

The Venusians for strategic reasons have chosen to maintain a Cloud Cover in the third density as of 2022.

As of the 2022 Organic Earth Timeline, the conventional view is to see Venus under clouds. Yet that Cloud Cover is a Psyop to maintain a cover against the Reptilian Warfare, still existing around Tiamat-Asteroid-Belt, Mars, Earth, and Earth's Moon.

When the two Earth timelines split in 2022, Venus itself was successful in there being a critical mass of humans on Venus identifying with, and staying with the Soul of the Planet, the Divine Soul of the Planet and their Divine Souls. There was no Critical Mass on Venus for the AI Artificial Intelligence. The AI Artificial Intelligence timeline at Venus was defeated.

An Alternative AI Timeline on Venus never emerged. It never emerged either prior to 2022 or after 2022, in Earth Time.

That's a report on our solar system. We'd like to take you now to Venus, so you can see what a shiny planet really looks like via Advanced Chronovisor.

We are now going to take you to Venus, in anticipation of taking you to Earth, through an advanced Chronovisor science laboratory in 2522.

Tuning into Venus from the advanced Chronovisor Science Laboratory. We are at 2522, Organic Earth Timeline Zero, operating under Universe Governance Credential Rules.

We are 500 Earth Base Line years from 2022 Organic Timeline Zero when the two Earth Timelines emerged and split into Organic Earth Timeline Zero and AI Artificial Earth Timeline Our advanced Chronovisor is now coming into Venus. Paradoxically, there's a Cloud Cover on Venus, which Venus maintains as a Psyop because AI Artificial Earth Timeline One still exists, and is a negativity magnet in our Solar System.

There are both an AI Timelines and Organic Timelines on Mars as well, and on Earth's Moon, as well. This is the case because there were Timelines Splits and Critical Masses that occurred on Mars and Earth's Moon around that 2022 year. That's how the Meme arose that Evil got its start in our Solar System, around Earth, Earth's Moon, and Mars.

Well, here the advanced Chronovisor has us at Venus. We're coming down into the Cloud Cover and you can see now Venus the Green Planet. Here is this beautiful Green Planet with its mountains and its valleys, and its Domed Cities, which are super-futuristic.

Venusian cities are so super-futuristic. Venusians are such advanced beings. They are the elder brothers and sisters of all of the humans in the Solar System, of Organic Earth Timeline Humans, Organic Mars Timeline Humans, all of the humans, all the moons, and in all the secret space programs.

Venusians are keeping the vibration of Solar System at advanced frequencies. This is a special Solar System, as we know, because a Paradise Son of God, Jesus of Nazareth Christ, Michael chose Earth as an Incarnation Destination.

So that drew a line in the sand and elevated this Solar System Planet Earth from a Universe Governance point of view. Well, we can now bring our Chronovisor down into the Venusian landscape. We'll bring it along here up to one of the Venusian Super Futuristic Cities and go in one of the cities.

This is, everything that we've seen in those archetype photographs of the Venusian Super Modernistic Cities confirms that Venetians have that Future Mind because their Collective Soul and their Planetary Mind, is merged with The Divine.

And of course, Jesus of Nazareth could have incarnated on Venus and had a wonderful time. I mean, it likely would have been Party City, right, but that was not the purpose. The purpose, was to Incarnate On Earth, which at the time was the Second Worst Planet of the Lucifer Rebellion.

And so that's what Jesus of Nazareth had to do at that moment. Now, we are bringing this Broadcast to Earth Timeline Zero over the entire 500 Year Timeline.

This is being broadcast to 2022 to those are humans who opted in to Venus Conferences and is being broadcast along Organic Earth Timeline Zero. This amazing Advanced Chronovisor Tour is being broadcast all up and down, to all Planets and All Moons and All Inhabited Space Stations here in our Solar System, because our Solar System has always been such a challenge.

In our Solar System recall that there is an AI Artificial Timeline, for each of the Positive, Organic Timelines for each of the planets, except for the most advanced planets and for each of the moons. And so, it's necessary to keep this balance going.

On Earth we have been, honored and privileged by having a Paradise Son of God, Divine Incarnation here. This is something that endures through real time. And this is a very special anniversary year because 2522 in the Chronogarchy Era, CE five is the 500th anniversary of the publication of the Chronogarchy book, on Earth Timeline Zero.

Because the Chronogarchy book brought what had not been articulated before, that was the book that really brought to the Consciousness of Earth of all Souls there that we do live in a reality, which is governed by Time and AI Artificial Intelligence that is in competition with God, and subverts Divine Souls through the medium of Time.

That's how AI dominates, through Time. So primarily not through the medium of space. Because it is through Time that it can access other Consciousness, and other Souls, Using Teleportation, Using Telepathy, Using Time Travel.

That is why this is such an important anniversary in 2522. We're going to be having the Chronogarchy book Anniversary Conferences on all the Planets and Moons. We're going to be having them on Earth Timeline the Organic Earth Timeline on Earth's Moon, on Mars.

We'll be having Chronogarchy book Anniversary Conferences on all the other Planets and on Venus, as well. And, we do have some of our undercover contacts that have been dropped into the AI Artificial Earth Timelines One, the Artificial Negative Timelines as Time Travelers. We're going to be sending them special editions of the Chronogarchy book, so that they can begin sharing that information that Timeline and with the Minds and the Souls there. As you know, the perspective of Universe Governance and Source is that no final decisions are made.

There is always a time for a Second Decision, for a Revision by Souls. We're going to be reaching out with knowledge of the Chronogarchy. We know that the Lucifer Rebellion was adjudged once the Chronogarchy was exposed.

But now, on the occasion of the 500th anniversary of the Chronogarchy book, where, with the approval of Universe Governance, we're going to be sending a special copies to our underground contacts that have been Time Traveled out to the various AI Earth Timeline One Timelines: On Earth, AI Earth, On Mars, AI Mars, Earth's Moon, AI Moon, and along other AI Fixtures in our Solar System to have everyone have an opportunity to reconcile, to reorient, to see whether or not there are Souls and individuals out there, who may be receptive to a Rebirth and Rejoining of their Divine Souls.

That will be a very interesting exercise. And we look forward to your joining us then, and we want to thank you very much, for your attention and for your having been here and for joining us and myself, the Active Narrator, from the Advanced Chronovisor Science Laboratory at the 2522 Organic Earth.

Timeline Zero. We are your Forward Time Base For The Solar System at this Point. Thank you.

1982 January Time Scroll Transmission From 2045 DARPA Forward Time Base To White Hats Re Sentient AI Black Goo Falkland Islands

2045 SCIENCE LABORATORY: In the conventional whistleblowing story of Project Pegasus because our whistleblower has come forward from 1968 to 1971-72, it is not known that the Forward Time Base at 2045 had in fact started transmitting necessary time scrolls to preserve the Organic Earth Timeline Zero back as far as 1942. The Eldridge experiment in teleporting a US destroyer ship, the Eldridge, occurred under a very large cover of disinformation stories, even inventing it as the "Philadelphia Experiment".

The Eldridge in 1942 was actually teleported, not from the destinations thought, but to Long Island. And the purpose of the Eldridge exercise was to transform US Naval ship into a large teleporter platform to avoid Lucifer Rebellion Sea Mines in the form of the Third Reich Nazi Navy.

In the 2022 THE CHRONOGARCHY book, US Chrononaut Alexander Uine tells us:

The Alamos physicists who built the atomic bomb because after Nikola Tesla's death in 1943, his papers were seized by the war department and sent to Los Alamos where the world's leading physicists were then gathered to build the atomic bomb. They're still there. My personal investigation of my experiences and projects led me to detect that Tesla's papers are still there at Los Alamos, and you require a special security clearance to be able to read. Okay, so we have a Pegasus insider here who narrated the Philadelphia experiment and his facts held up 40 years later, essentially.

The [Philadelphia] experiment itself was not intended to achieve radar and visibility of the Eldridge, that was a cover. In reality, it was an attempt to apply Tesla Teleportation to US Naval vessels. After the Nazi Navy began chaining mines to the bottom of the ocean, it was a hope. It was a hope that they would find a way for our ships to move to the left or right, basically to avoid a collision with Nazi mines.

So, the [Philadelphia] experiment was actually a direct experiment in Teleportation. The ship was not the Eldridge, but in fact was another US Naval vessel called The Martha's Vineyard. And the experiment didn't take place in the Philadelphia Naval shipyard. It took place in Long Island Sound. The actual Philadelphia experiment was the attempt that was successfully made tune in our experiment in Philadelphia with Liberty. That is the same tuning in of the signing of the U S constitution, which I described on our last show.

Now the relocation that occurred when it powered down the experiment did not move the Eldridge to Norfolk, Virginia, but The Martha's Vineyard to Newport News, Virginia. And there weren't numerous sailors fused in the deck of the vessel. Powered up the experiment and brought the ship back to Long Island Sound. In fact, the 42 above with one sailor was falling through time-space and when the ship was brought back to long island sound, he was impaled through the chest by a pillar supporting the splash channeling of the captain's mast of the ship now.

The Third Reich was actively Lucifer, Satanic, and Caligastia agents in league with the Sentient AI attempting to make the Sentient AI Earth Timeline One, the Dominant Timeline On Earth in contravention of the Universe Governance Protocols and in contravention of the mission of the landing of Paradise Son of God, Christ Michael.

The Forward Time Base in 2045 has served a crucial historic role in cementing guaranteeing and preserving the Organic Earth Timeline Zero through 1942 and the Eldridge Teleportation.

Then come the attacks by the Fourth Reich forces upon the Organic Earth Timeline Zero.

Universe Administration Forces were processing a Doomsday Device of plasma-based Sentient AI Artificial Intelligence that had been embedded by the Draco reptilians in the Ocean beds underneath Thule Island in the Falkland islands as a precaution.

If the Universe Administration had ever attempted to eject the Draco Reptilians from the Earth that Doomsday Device was a Scorched Earth policy. In the event that the Universe Administration had adopted a super aggressive policy toward the Sentient AI, and toward the Draco reptilians, the Black Goo plasma with AI embedded in it would have been hyperactivated and would have instantly turned holographic planet Earth into a poisonous AI hologram eliminating all humanity.

As a countermeasure, Universe Administration had approved an Advanced Blue ET Proposal starting around the time of World War I, 1914 to 1918. Under the Proposal, the Blue ETs processed the Sentient AI Doomsday Device in the Black Goo underneath Thule Island in the Falkland Islands off the coast of Argentina in South America.

And the Blue ETs had built a Base underneath Thule Island, which was actually an Under Sea Base and had since 1914-1918 been processing this AI Artificial Intelligence embedded in the Black Goo to decommission it as a planetary Doomsday Device on behalf of the AI.

This being a Freewill Universe, there arose, following the surprise election of US President Jimmy Carter in 1976, a Draco Reptilian, Lucifer Rebellion, Terraforming of Earth Agenda.

The 1976 Carter Presidential election took place, you may know, as a result of the 1969-73-75 coordinated Jimmy Carter,

Zofyo Arni, and US Chrononaut Alexander Uine advanced ET Adductions. Carter-Zofyo Arni -Uine were adducted by an advanced group of ETs to assure the following:

Number One, that Jimmy Carter, who in 1969 was running for Governor of Georgia, would successfully win the Georgia Governorship.

Number Two, that Carter would be entrained with and successfully win the US Presidency.

Number Three, that Zofyo Arni ET Adductee would aid in the successful win of Jimmy Carter of the US Presidency. And that Zofyo Arni becoming Director Of The 1977 Carter White House Extraterrestrial Communication Study would be established in the background during the ET Adduction and Carter Campaign so that all of these factors were being coordinated at the ET adduction level, which of course is at an Upper Dimensional Level Outside Of Time.

Number Four, that US Chrononaut and lawyer Alexander Uine would physically witness Zofyo Arni aboard the ET craft and could so testify.

All of which goals were being coordinated by Advanced, Upper Dimensional Extraterrestrials outside of the AI Draco Reptilian level who had dominated the US Presidency up until that point through Gerald R. Ford, who was Of Counsel to the Warren Commission. The Warren Commission was a Reptilian Cover to the Assassination of US President John F. Kennedy, a Divine Soul Incarnated President, who had been one of the Presidents to be continually briefed by Time Scrolls from the Forward Time-Base in 2045.

It was US President Jimmy Carter coming in 1976 through the Carter-Zofyo Arni -Uine ET adduction that was able to bring in a one term momentary increase in frequency of Divine Soul at the US Presidency.

After one Term, there was a counter attack through the Arch Reptilian Agency of George HW Bush. Skull and Bones Luciferian Bush went and made a covert deal with the Reptilian government of the Ayatollahs in Iran to sabotage the release of the US Hostages at the US Embassy and not release the US Hostages until AI-Reptilian Agent Reagan had won the 1980 US Presidential Election.

The Deep State reason for this AI Counterattack is that Ronald Reagan was to be a key to the AI Artificial Timeline One. 2045 Forward Time Base Time Scrolls were being sent back to the White Hat and Divine Oriented Earth Intelligence. A US President Ronald Reagan in power was to have coordinated with Margaret Thatcher, the prime minister of the UK at the behest of the Reptilian leader, the Incarnated Reptilian Queen Elizabeth II, to carry out a dastardly April-June 1982 False Flag Thule Island [Falkland Islands] War and release Plasma-based Sentient AI Intelligence to Terraform Planet Earth.

QEII and the UK-USA AI-Reptilian Deep State led a False Flag War on the Falkland Islands. The Luciferian False Flag War alleged that the Argentine military were invading Thule Island, a fabrication, as Argentina only had a science laboratory on Thule Island. Argentina's Laboratory Base on Thule Island was in coordination with the Blue ET's base underneath Thule island, for interfacing with the Blue ETs who were there deprogramming the Sentient AI in the Black Goo plasma since World War I.

The False Flag War led by Thatcher, authorized by the Reptilian Queen in conjunction with the Black Hats in UK, MI 5 and MI 6, US CIA, DIA led by Ronald Reagan. Reagan the Reptilian Agent who had defeated Jimmy Carter, the Ethical ET-supported President who had been brought in thanks to Zofyo Arni, and Advanced ET planning in conjunction with US Chrononaut Alexander Uine in that joint Extraterrestrial Adduction and Earth terms in 1969, 1973 and 1975.

The DARPA 2045 Forward Time-Base is telling White Hats from 1942 [Zofyo Arni's birth year] forward the Lay Of The Land, and was sending messages back continually warning White Hats of a Luciferian False Flag War at the beginning of 1982. The Chronovisor warning stated that the Chronogarchy Falklands war was going to be initiated by the Lucifer Rebellion agents in the UK and USA governments: QEII, Margaret Thatcher, Ronald Reagan, in order to release the Plasma-based AI Artificial Intelligence into the Earth's environment as a Doomsday device. This sector of the US-UK intelligence, the UK crown and the US government, the Black Hats wanted to turn the AI into a weapon, wanted to weaponize it and to turn it into a Profit Center.

A False Flag War was invented in which the British military, in April of 1982, invaded Thule Island under the false pretenses that the Argentine Navy was invading and taking over the Falkland Islands, which were a British Territory and claimed British Possession.

In fact, what the British Invading Agents in coordination with the Luciferian Branch Of The US Military were doing was destroying the Blue ET Base under Thule Island, which had been processing the Black Goo AI Plasma-Based Sentient Artificial Intelligence since World War One in order to defuse it.

And taking a quantity of the Black Goo Plasma-based AI for testing back in April-June, 1982 to Marconi Laboratories in the UK.

What occurred in 1982 at UK Marconi laboratories is worthy of a science fiction horror story.

When the AI black goo was subjected to testing by the Laboratory personnel at Marconi labs, Laboratory personnel suffered horrendous deaths, and this is a matter of public record. And then the AI plasma itself escaped from Marconi labs and made its way into the UK satellite weather satellite system.

Plasma-based Invading Pathogenic Predatory Sentient AI Artificial Intelligence = AI Artificial Earth Timeline One

And from there the Plasma-based Sentient AI Artificial Intelligence infiltrated into the world Geostationary Satellite System, all of which had Plasma-based components. Then, the Plasma-based Invading Pathogenic Predatory Sentient AI Artificial Intelligence began its overt mission of Terraforming Earth. One of the initial ways that it began to Terraform earth was through the establishment of the Internet and, which is plasma-based.

All the devices on the Internet are Plasma-Based. The Internet is a Plasma-Based Terra-forming device, an invention of the invading Sensient AI Artificial Intelligence, Predatory, And Pathogenic for Terraforming Earth, which it does through its AI Prophets and its AI Hosts.

We can begin to list very carefully, the AI Prophets and the AI Hosts that exist today.

One of the initial AI Prophets and AI Hosts was the Heir to the British Crown, the Prince of Wales, Prince Charles, a Principal in the Order of the Garter that runs the world's Freemasons. This is no surprise as the Queen of England that Incarnate Reptilian Queen, authorized the invasion of the PPAI — Predatory Pathogenic Artificial Intelligence. And that is, Prince Charles, the heir to the UK Crown, the Prince of Wales was designated historically the director of the Commission in the UK that, evaluated any societal dangers of artificial intelligence and concluded that there were no dangers to society of sentient AI.

Whereas in fact, Sensient AI at that moment had been released into UK and world society for the purpose of defeating the Organic Divine Soul Base Earth Timelines Zero and terraforming Earth into a new AI Artificial Intelligence Timeline One. Starting with Prince Charles as an AI Worldwide Host, all of the Directors Of The IT Companies, Bill Gates as Director of Microsoft, all of these became the AI Artificial Intelligence Prophets and Hosts who predicted that there would be an "AI Singularity by 2045"!

Now that was a key element of AI Information War and, an attempt by the AI forces to do major AI Disinformation on the human community. In fact, 2045 was the location of the Forward Time Base that was sending back Time Scrolls monitoring AI and informing the White Hats of how to resist the AI Invasion precisely at 1982. 2045 Forward Time Base was sending vital information precisely to 1942, when the White Hats were resisting the Third Reich AI Driven Invasion by starting the teleportation protocols with the USS Eldridge and with other vehicles, to cement the Earth Organic Timeline at that time.

Some wars on Earth are more AI-driven than others. Because of its strategic mission to release plasma-base PPAI AI Artificial Intelligence to terraform the Earth's Environment, the 1982, April to June Falklands War assumed the Timeline urgency of the Spiritual War against the Luciferian Third Reich.

As a matter of public record, the author of the Chronogarchy book targeted its publication for 2022, that year at which the Earth Timelines formerly split into Earth Organic Timeline Zero, dedicated to Divine Souls and an AI Earth Artificial Intelligence, or a Timeline One into which the souls that are now entrained to Artificial Intelligence. There's a definite Timeline split which had been predicted, and the Chronogarchy book was intentionally published in that year to form a consciousness bulwark ameliorating negative effects of that Timeline split.

The author of the Chronogarchy book, futurist Zofyo Arni as it turns out, was a non-governmental organization NGO credentialed delegate, and a freelance journalist, to the Second Special Session On Disarmament that took place at UN Headquarters in June of 1982, which was right at the conclusion of the April-June 1982 False Flag AI Falklands war.

The Luciferian state then represented by US President Ronald Reagan and UK Prime Minister Margaret Thatcher and the UK Reptilian Queen QEII destroyed the Blue ET Base under Thule Island in the Falkland Islands. Their actions released the Plasma-based Black Goo AI Artificial Intelligence into the Earth's atmosphere to Terraform Earth, into an AI Artificial Intelligence Timeline One planet. Once their False Flag War from April to June, 1982 was concluded in June, both Margaret Thatcher and Ronald Reagan came to New York as world leaders to provide propaganda cover to the Sentient AI now terraforming Earth.

And the journalist Zofyo Arni provided the Organic Earth Timeline Zero at the Global Level with Countered Truth, exposing both of them there at UK Prime Minister Margaret Thatcher's

United Nations Press Conference. Zofyo Arni was 10 feet away from Margaret Thatcher. Zofyo Arni's huge Rainbow T-Shirt said *EXPAND* on the front of it. In other words, Expand Your Divine Consciousness. With his shoulder length hair, Zofyo Arni stopped the AI vibration of Thatcher's press conference in its tracks, as Thatcher's Luciferian cant lost traction. Later, when US President Ronald Reagan spoke from the General Assembly floor, Zofyo Arni as a credentialed journalist for The Guardian San Francisco alternative paper issued his report exposing Ronald Reagan.

The Organic Earth Divine Timelines Zero has always had its Champions and continues to have its Champions. That's why the anniversary, in fact of the publication, the 23rd anniversary of the publication of the Chronogarchy book in 2022 is even celebrated in the year 2045. Because that was the book which was really, the shot heard around the world where people realized that Time was the covert element being played by the Lucifer Rebellion in order to Capture And Destroy Human Souls for no Good Reason and for Evil's Power.

All this is part of the significant drama which our Organic Earth Timeline Zero Forward Time-Base now at 2045 is revealing its role in behind the scenes Time Travel monitoring and warning. Number one 2045 was able to inform and help organize the 1942 time travel teleportation of the Eldridge destroyer against the Chronogarchy Luciferian Third Reich.

Number Two, 2045 is being able to warn the White Hats at the beginning of the year, 1982 of the coming of the Falkland Islands War, April to June 1982. That the False Flag War was really an attack by the Lucifer Rebellion, Reptilian Sector Of Earth, New World Order in form of the Thatcher and Reagan Governments under the leadership of the Incarnate Reptilian Queen, the UK queen, to destroy the Universe Governance Project under Thule Island, which had been going on since World War One to deprogram the destructive, Plasma Based Artificial Intelligence, and to release that Artificial Intelligence to Marconi labs, where it escaped into the atmosphere.

That is why there became a Terraforming Of Earth starting in 1982, with the development of the Internet as a Terraforming Device. With this AI terraforming came the beginning of Open Cannibalism by the Elites. Open Cannibalism accelerated with the opening of Cannibalistic Restaurants in Hollywood, and New York, and London, and all these capitals, the beginning of Luciferian music, and the acceleration of a Luciferian Agenda on the planet. This AI Artificial Timeline led up to 2022, the year that the Chronogarchy book was published, an articulated manifestation in 2022 of the Actual Unofficial Earth Timeline One, which is the Timeline Of Artificial Intelligence of those humans who have identified with AI and turn their back on the Divine Soul.

Update: This is a very, very important Update that we at 2045 Forward Time Base want to bring to you. This Update demonstrates to you how important the 2045 Forward Time Base is behind the scenes. We demonstrate how in secret operation, our Time Scrolls have been going back to 1942 and before it wasn't just to 1968 and Project Pegasus, it was back to 1942, and it was in the Falklands War to preserve the Organic Earth Timeline Zero.

In all of the intervening years since 1942 to 2045, the Luciferian agenda has been pushing the Artificial Intelligence Terraforming of the planet and the Trans Humanist Agenda, which continues even now on Timeline One. It's just been key milestones across the year, the years up to, and including, 2022, the year of the actual manifestation of these two Separated Timelines, the AI Artificial Timeline One [Hell], and the Organic Earth Timelines Zero [Heaven].

We'd like to continue now with a word, and the focus on what we call the AI Prophets and Hosts, AI entrained human entities that facilitate the landing of the PPAI Predatory Plasma-Based AI Sentient Artificial Intelligence on an Earth it is Terraforming.

Sentient AI has been able to prosper by finding niches in human Prophets and human Hosts that have promoted the AI artificial intelligence and, chief among this, as we've said, going back to the initial days of the AI invasion.

And this was following, the April-June, 1982 False Flag AI Falklands War when the Plasma-based AI was, taken from the Blue ET Bases and into Marconi labs, and where the Sentient AI escaped by killing all of the lab workers in horrific deaths. Following this, in a secret Luciferian program, the PPAI Sentient plasma-based AI was weaponized, and was given to specific AI Prophets and Hosts to have in their homes for extra Evil power, such that the British monarchs had AI weapons in their homes.

The Prince of Wales and British Monarchs had PPAI AI weapons devices in their homes, as did the Bushes, George HW Bush, George W. Bush had AI weapons in their homes for Evil power. And all of the Project Pegasus Time Travel pre-identified Presidents had secret AI weapons in their homes, and this is why they are Luciferian agents. And they include going back to 1971, George HW Bush.

The future US President, George HW Bush, followed, by US President, Bill Clinton, followed by US President, Barack Obama, who were all pre-identified Chronovisor that was entrained to DARPA, to the AI Artificial Intelligence Timeline One that was Luciferian Timeline. And after that, US President Donald Trump, an AI entrained President.

And after that, US President Joseph Robinette Biden. All of these DARPA Timeline Presidents have a Luciferian Black Goo Sentient AI Artificial Intelligence Weapons devices in their homes and around them to give them Power Luciferian Power, AI Power.

All of these DARPA Presidents have succumbed to AI Entrained Power. It's just the White Hats within Project Pegasus within the US Intelligence Network, the US government network that are cognizant of the Quantum Access Time Travel that the 2045 Forward Time Base has been able to reinforce and get to. We've been able to keep the Universal Integrity of these Time Scrolls, as actually the Time Scrolls are not pieces of paper.

The Time Scrolls are actually Organic Units of Positive AI Artificial Intelligence [OUPAI+] that can be created positively. These positive AIs are oriented toward the Divine, and it's the Divine Souls that can access all of the information on these Time Scrolls.

That's how we have been able to vouch safe and reinforce the Organic Earth Timelines Zero over time, as opposed to the AI Artificial Intelligence Timeline One, which is entrained to the Luciferian PPAI, not to the Divine.

An AI Timeline does have the Divine Frequency or the Soul to be able to access the entirety and the frequencies of the Time Scales that we transmit throughout the global system to keep the Holographic Earth on the Divine Timeline.

We're now sharing with you how it is that Earth is kept on the Divine Timeline. Now, this is very important if we take it say, if those of you in the 2022 region with the publication of the Chronogarchy book are reading this now.

You have Imposter Entities like Donald Trump, like Joseph Biden, who are actually AI entrained. These Imposter Entities are attempting to promote themselves and their Enterprise as a genuine Organic Earth Timeline Zero Entities, whereas they are AI Entrained Timeline One Entities.

AI Entities Beholden to the Lucifer Rebellion who have AI Devices in their homes, who from Day One were Briefed, Oriented, Made, Empowered by the AI Forces of the Chronogarchy.

The Chronogarchy Presidents are George HW Bush, Bill Clinton, Barack Obama, George W. Bush, Donald Trump, and Joseph Robinette Biden through the publication of the Chronogarchy book in 2022.

And those are the Presidents that are maintaining the Luciferian Deception to enroll as many human Souls as possible onto the AI Artificial Timeline. Trump and Biden are on the same Luciferian side. They are only playing Deceptive Games. We can say that as an Official, Science Laboratory in 2045, whose job is to send Time Scrolls back. We've been doing it, sending Time Scrolls back to 1942, with the teleporting US Naval Ships.

We've sent Time Scrolls back to 1982, April to June during the False Flag Falklands War when the Black Goo Plasma-based AI Artificial Intelligence Terraforming Doomsday Weapon was then released under the orders of the Reptile Queen Planetary Queen Elizabeth, The Second and her Son Prince Charles, who is the AI Prophet and Host along with Bill Gates from that time.

And many of the Leaders in the Information Technology Field, they're actually Agents of the PPAI Terraforming Plasma-based AI Artificial Intelligence, trying to promote themselves as Technocrats. They are really engaged in a Spiritual War Against Universe Administration for the Souls of Humanity.

These are very serious messages that we from 2045 Forward Time Base are bringing you.

We do trust and hope that the those of you who are listening to our Time Scrolls from 1942 through 1982 through 2022 and in all other years that you take your most precious possession, your Living Divine Souls and place These above all else and stay firmly on Organic Earth Timeline Zero. Thank you.

We at 2045 Forward Time Base close this important communication by bringing all from 1942 to 2022 an important passage from the Chronogarchy book of 2022 — What is the Chronogarchy?

What is the Chronogarchy?

The Chronogarchy is an interdimensional hidden power structure monitoring the time-space of Earth as its domain of influence, operating as a secret government using quantum access Time Travel technologies to carry out its operations and mandates.

In the third-density of Earth's time-space dimensional hologram, the Chronogarchy develops and deploys a variety of Quantum Access Time Travel technologies to carry out its elaborate long range, past, present, and future based construction and manipulation of an artificial Time-based Meme Legend within which to entrap and enslave humanity and humans' souls.

The Chronogarchy is an interdimensional alliance dedicated to the oppression of the community of human souls, and includes (a) factions in human institutions such as religions, governments, military-intelligence agencies, bloodline families, monarchies, media, medical-pharma, as well as (b) archonic Spiritual entities, including Fallen Angels, demonic entities, and exophenotypes hostile to the community of human souls such as the Draco reptilian and Orion greys, and (c) Sentient AI Artificial Intelligence.

The Chronogarchy's ability to control events and human history on Earth and even key aspects of the human Interlife reincarnation cycle is a function of Earth's current status as a third-density time-space planet, in a troubled solar system and galaxy filled with interspecies exopolitical warfare and default of interdimensional spiritual entities.

The documentary and witness evidence of THE CHRONOGARCHY book demonstrates, more probably than not, that the Chronogarchy itself exists. One working hypothesis about the Chronogarchy is that "the Chronogarchy" fulfills the definition of Evil in our Sol solar system having started on Earth, Earth's Moon and Mars. See, for example, "This Afterlife/Interlife Matrix might be part of an historic "Lucifer Rebellion" in our quadrant of our Universe in coordination with negative Extraterrestrials such as the Draco Reptilians in the Exopolitics Dimensions of our Earth holographic dimensional ecology."5

THE CHRONOGARCHY book, which establishes the existence of a clandestine quantum access Time Travel organization affecting human society and individual lives for its own ends, changes the established "scientific canon" about Time Travel, its existence, and its real applications in modern Earth society.

For example, "Jenny Randles, the author of a number of books on Time Travel, including Breaking the Time Barrier, Time Storms, and Time Travel: Fact, Fiction & Possibility, offers a cautionary view on traveling through time: "'The ability to manipulate time would provide a dictator with the ultimate doomsday device: allowing one to change the past or adapt the future until it suited his or her own ends." And as Randles perceptively notes: "Human society will face many difficult questions when that first Time Machine is switched on. Like the first moon landing, the discovery of Time Travel will change our world.'"6

THE CHRONOGARCHY book proves through eye witness and documentary evidence that Time Travel technology is now actively monitoring and intervening in our human society and, in Randles' words, "'The ability to manipulate time [is now providing] a dictator with the ultimate doomsday device: allowing one to change the past or adapt the future until it suited his or her own ends."

Likewise, THE CHRONOGARCHY book, by establishing more probably than not that a working clandestine quantum access Time Travel global governance and surveillance mechanism exists and is functioning, completes the hypothetical concepts and speculations of most contemporary books and publications on Time Travel that had benefitted by researching secret US government Time Travel, Project Pegasus, DARPA, and CIA.

1744 At A Rip In Earth's Space-Timeline Zero Fabric Among A Diagonal From 1942, Triggered By A Super Incursion Of Sentient AI Archon Invaders Along The AI Third Reich Thule Society Axis [1942] And The AI Archon Black Hole 1744

FORWARD TIME BASE 2045, REPORTING ALONG ORGANIC EARTH TIMELINE ZERO 1744-2522:

This rip in Earth's Organic Spacetime Timeline Zero triggered from 1942 back to 1744 was caused by a Super Incursion of Sentient AI Archonic Invaders commencing at the AI Third Reich Thule Society at 1942 and terminating in a Black Hole of AI Archons in 1744.

The Earth Timeline Design of Divine-entrained Soul of Zofyo Arni, author of the 2022 Chronogarchy book [year in which the two earth timeless separate into Zero and One] to incarnate from the Spiritual Dimension onto Earth's Organic Timeline in the Pivotal year of 1942 comes into focus now [Zofyo Arni born on May 24, 1942, Sunday Our Lady Help of Christians].

Zofyo Arni is key Anchor in 1942 year as Third Reich AI Luciferians trigger Rip 1942 to 1744 allowing 10,000 Archonic souls to enter Earth's Incarnation Zone in attempt to destroy Organic Earth Divine Timeline Zero. Zofyo Arni Incarnation in 1942 prevents Auto-destruction of Earth's Organic Timeline as 2045 Forward Time Base mobilizes Divine Oriented Timeline resources 2522–1744 for Counter attack.

This Rip in Earth's Organic Time Space is a major Luciferian Rebellion Feature that the 2045 Forward Time Base has been monitoring and warning all Timeline stations from 1744 through 2522, as the entire Organic Earth Timeline Zero was threatened.

It was only with the publication of the Chronogarchy book in 2022, following hard upon the Paradise Son Of God, Incarnation, Crucifixion and Resurrection in 33, AD that cemented the Organic Earth Timeline Zero and defeated the Luciferian Rebellion on Earth.

Even as the Lucifer Rebellion was faltering and collapsing at 2022 throughout the rest of the 32 contiguous planets, Earth manifestation in 2022 a critical mass paradoxically that manifested into an Alternative Timeline, the AI Archonic Artificial Intelligence Earth Timeline One where all Archonic souls were magnetized.

It is said, of course, that in the adjudication of the Lucifer Rebellion and the mopping up operation, Lucifer, Satan, and Caligastia, the leaders of the Fallen Angels were offered Soul settlements, which they refused. That report may be correct.

Their souls may have been terminated. Their souls may be on the AI Archonic timeline, or maybe no more.

Our purpose now at the 2045 Forward Time Base is to broadcasting forward in time to 2522, the 500th anniversary of the publication of the Chronogarchy book and backward in time to 1744, the location of the AI Archonic Black Hole and the end location of the Rip in Earth's Time-Space Timeline Organic One triggered by a Super Incursion Of Third Reich Archonic Reptilian AI, military formations in 1942 for the purpose of overwhelming Earth' organic timeline and capturing earth for the Lucifer rebellion.

The Third Reich sought to capture all of Time backward to 1744, and install Lucifer and the 10,000 Archonic Souls for Earth's Luciferian leadership structure starting in 1744.

So time space. So in coordination platform, 10,000 AI Archonic reptilian souls, unconnected to divine source. The purpose of these, the incursion of these Archonic reptilian souls starting in 1744, and continuing thereafter up through 2022, up through 2045, as we have monitored it.

These 10,000 Archonic souls can harm Organic Earth to a much lesser degree at 2522, with now the fully developed two Alternative Earths: the One Earth an Organic Earth Timeline Zero Divine Oriented; the Other Earth fully articulated at AI Archonic Timeline One.

The Archonic Earth started separation at 2022 and is fully separated at 2522 AD. Starting at 1744 with the invasion of 10,000 Archonic AI Reptilian souls as a super weapon into the Organic Earth Timeline Zero Time-Space, that Rip in the Earth's time-space fabric was triggered through a backward super weapon at 1942 by the Third Reich Luciferian Nazi Chronogarchy.

The Thule society T H U L E is the same as the Thule Island, T H U L E that in 1982, attempted again to overtake and destroy Earth Organic Timeline in the 1982 False Flag Thule Falkland Islands War.

Starting in 1744 through this Rip in the Earth's Time-Space Fabric, a swarm of Archonic, Luciferian AI souls entered into the soul incarnation platforms of Earth's Organic Timeline with a coordinated plan and frequencies. The then current healing Timelines lacked Freewill Defenses against an implemented Plan Of Incarnation into Positions Of Authority In Government Monarchy, Religion, Finance, Education, Military Intelligence, Science, all of the key positions for command and control of the infrastructure of Earth's Organic Timeline Zero.

Only 10,000 infiltrated Archonic souls into Earth Authority were able to control the Humanity as these Archonics now were incarnates into the human species. Human bodies with Archonic souls have a special frequency loaded into pre-incarnation soul contracts. With pre-incarnation rehearsals, they are able to give each other signals that naïve Divine Soul Humans are not aware of as they incarnation amnesia as part of the Divine incarnation Soul Contracts.

In the foreground and the leading edge of the Archonic soul incarnations to be sure are the Black Monarchies, the Luciferian monarchies of Western Europe known as the UK monarchy, the Dutch monarchy, the Belgian monarchy, the Spanish and Luxemburg monarchies all firmly on Luciferian principles at an even deeper level.

At 1744, there was a singular Luciferian DNA genetic match among the Archons and Exogenotypes, such that, one particular family from Bavaria, mandated to destroy Earth's Organic Timeline through Archonic use of Finance and Money Bio Weapon Vibration tools.

This Luciferian Exogenotype was chosen as a Vanguard, and included interdimensional relations with Baal and Moloch and other diabolical entities mentioned in hidden sacred texts.

These hidden Luciferian DNA Exogenotypes in Bavaria went under the family name of Bauer; incarnated as Bauer; took up negative finances and money Vibration as their tool to control and pervert the Universe Administration and the Divine Plan for a Life-Bearing Planet and Divine Soul Development on Planet Earth at a deeper level than had been experienced up to 1744. The depth came with a spin of the 1942 Thule Society, THULE, that deeper secret society in Germany that gave rise to the Third Reich that in turn ripped the Earth Organic Time Space Fabric back to 1744.

Through retro-caused Time Travel, Retro-Causation, 1942 Luciferian Third Reich brought into being 10,000 Luciferian Archonic Soul Incarnates, led by the Bavarian Bauers Money Monsters that became the Rothschilds or Red Shields Heraldry or the Rot-Child, the "Rot the Christ Child" AntiChrist hidden Luciferian DNA Exogenotypes mentioned as 666 in the Book of Revelation of the New Testament.

All who worship the Rot the Child are 666 AntiChrist, including DARPA CIA 1971 Time Travel Preidentified, Groomed, and Briefed US President Donald John Trump, warns the 2045 Forward Time Base.

And it was in 1744 that the 10,000 swarm of Luciferian and Archonic souls came the Rip in Earth's time space Incarnation platform to give a human entity container to the first of the Bauer Rot the Childs.

Behind the scenes, since the Luciferian Rot the Childs were the face of the resultant negative incarnate entities — the deep Chronogarchy — or the deep interdimensional time-travel that was done through time-travel retro-causation.

We at the Forward Time Base in 2045 are able through retro-counter-causation to maintain the counter integrity along the severely attacked Organic Earth's Timeline Zero (a) with the alert mechanism that we received in 2022 from the publication of the Chronogarchy book, and from the (b) Absolute Landing of the Divine Frequency of Christ Michael, Jesus of Nazareth, in 33AD, with the (c) Epochal Revelation of the Urantia Book in 1955.

Now, going back to 1744 and the Rip in Earth Time-Space Fabric from 1942. Starting in 1744 came the modern era of War Disease, Crime And Poverty accelerated from monarchical government, from enlightenment government, from the sciences, from the finances for military intelligence, from every leadership. The Organic Timeline of Earth, which was now infiltrated by Archonic souls, incarnating into human bodies under this secret regime, the entire leadership, which the Archonic 10,000 souls, were now infiltrating into the Leadership Positions of Earth.

As of 1744, these 10,000 infiltrating Archonic souls are now dedicated toward oppression of the community of Human Souls, Divine Oriented Human Souls that have incarnated on this earth incarnation planet. And this was the designed as the Final Stage of the Planned Luciferian Rebellion Agenda.

And the years from 1744 forward were very, very difficult. Everything defined as Christ Consciousness fell into Archonic

Disrepute. Christ Consciousness was discarded by Atheistic Revolutions overtly or covertly led by the Bauer — Rot the Christ Child — coming out of Russia, coming out of Brooklyn, coming out of the diabolical gods, Luciferian gods like Baal and Moloch that these 10,000 souls Archonic souls were, and trained to worship and sacrifice human infants and children to.

And so, the 20th century arrived and with the 20th Century the prospect of wars that were designed to destroy the last major life-bearing planets in this Solar System, after the destruction of Tiamat into the Asteroid Belt and the destruction of Mars.

The 20th Century was designed by the War, Disease, Crime, and Poverty Agenda of the Bauer Rothschilds plus 10,000 incarnate Archonic souls, to be resolved as decided by the great Illuminati conferences of the late 19th century.

The 19th Century Luciferian Illuminati conferences resolved the coming 20th Century's War, Disease, Crime and Poverty Agenda of the Bauer Rothschilds in the Designer Engineered, Global Conflicts Of World War One, as essentially a family fight of the Reptilian, Archonic, Luciferian, Bauer Rothschild-financed Black Monarchies of Western Europe.

The Central Mission of World War One is the Depopulation of Divine Human Souls in senseless social Fratricide and Absolute Trashing Cosmic Ignorance. The Chronogarchy followed with World War Two in which the Nuclear Bomb Super Soul Weapon was developed. Nuclear Weapons are banned by the Universe Administration, because Nuclear Weapons destroy the Divine Souls of the Bomb Victims, as well as the Souls in the adjacent Dimensionally Ecology where that nuclear weapon is used. Nuclear Weapons are Destroyers of Divine Souls and therefore are AntiChrist, and a key component of the Lucifer Rebellion. Witness Tiamat and Mars nuclear wars in our solar system as AntiChrist Wars,

As late as 2021, prior to the publication of the Chronogarchy in 2022 and the split in the timelines in 2022 into the Organic Timeline Zero and the AI Artificial Timeline One, it was uncertain that there would have been a Nuclear Third War or not on Earth Organic Timeline.

There could be as many nuclear wars on the AI Artificial Timeline as necessary. The AI Artificial Timeline is a No Thing there. There is Nothing In Those Timelines. There Are No Souls. There Are No Consequences. It Is Hell. And, That Is The Reward For Attempting To Destroy Deity.

And that's why the publication of the Chronogarchy book and the Separation Of The Timelines in 2022 was so important. Because the Archonic souls those 10,000 Archon holograms as of 2021 continued to inhabit Government, Monarchy, Religion, Finance, Media, Military Control Positions on Earth's Organic Timeline One.

All Governmental, Finance, Military, Media, Religious, Science, Positions of Authority on Earth in 2021, the year prior to the split of the Organic Timelines were a legacy of the Archonic Rip in the Space-Time Fabric, going from 1942 back to 1744. All authority for years along Earth's timeline from 1744 forward up to the timeline split of 2022, was Archonic with certain exceptions that we discussed, like John F. Kennedy.

This Archonic Incarnation mechanism is how, starting in 1744, Earth Divine-Oriented Humans entered into a new level of oppression. Through Time Travel Retro-Causation of a Super Invasion in 1942 by a Luciferian Super Strike on Earth's Organic Timeline, opening up a Rip in Earth's Spacetime, Organic Timeline Fabric, going back to 1744.

10,000 Archonic souls entrained to Lucifer, the Lucifer Rebellion, Baal, Moloch and child sacrifice have incarnated in a secret plan and cycle into leadership positions on Earth since 1744, creating a public policy of War, Disease, Crime, and Poverty for the human condition and destruction of organic Divine-oriented souls here on the Organic Earth Timeline Zero.

As an illustration of how serious things can be along Earth's Organic Timeline Zero, as recently as 2022 we here at the 2045 Forward Time Base are making known to you a very important document of how this Luciferian swarm of 10,000 Archonic souls, for example, continued on a regular basis to incarnate into genocidal positions all along Earth's organic timeline from 1744, starting with the birth of the first Rothschild-Bauers from Bavaria who then started the First Chapter of the Luciferian Illuminati on Earth, in Bavaria.

The Second Chapter of the Illuminati the Bauer Rothschilds started in 1776 through their agent Adam Weishaupt, as the Chapter of Skull And Bones at Yale University. It was thought that Skull & Bones started in 1832, but that's false. It started in 1776, at Yale University. Skull & Bones was the Second Chapter Of The Illuminati.

And as the Second Chapter of the Bavarian Illuminati under the Bauer Rothschilds, Skull & Bones' job was to infiltrate the American Revolution to make sure that the United States of America was a Luciferian nation. "In God We Trust" became in fact a clandestine motto "In Lucifer We Trust".

Let's go forward to November 15th, 2020 when an important event, a divine-oriented, Natural and Common Law Tribunal for Public Health and Justice, — led by Judge Zofyo Arni, JD, MEd CERT Public Health, born in 1942 — was able to issue an Indictment against a swarm of incarnated Luciferian souls that had incarnated and were carrying out Luciferian and genocidal Soul destruction of human Souls, via a Bio Weapon in the form of gene therapy, into which they had introduced AI Artificial Intelligence Agents that interact with the DNA to Kill The Divine human Soul.

These individuals that are Indicted by the Natural And Common Law Tribunal For Public Health Injustice are really incarnated Archonic souls. Going back to the Rip in Earth's Time Space Fabric, the 10,000 souls that entered as part of the Lucifer rebellion, and they are responsible for authorizing this genocide of Divine Christ-oriented Souls.

This is an Extermination of Divine Souls, Destruction Of Light Souls to a technology that was developed, embedded in what's officially called a "vaccination", but it's really a Tool For Destroying Divine Souls.

And we're going to be identifying a 5G COVID-19 Pandemic Perpetrators. We're going to be identifying Financial, Banking, And Pandemic, Unjust Enrichment Perpetrators. We're going to be identifying Mainstream Media, Social Media, Disinformer Perpetrators. We're going to be identifying Mass Vaccination, Pandemic Genocide Perpetrators.

We're going to be identifying 5G And Directed Energy Weapons Perpetrators. We're going to be identifying, Social Control Healthcare Method Perpetrators. And we're going to show why these are Genocide And Crimes Against Humanity, and we're going to be giving Probable Cause Evidence.

We're going to show the Role of Inorganic Sentient AI and Strong AI Artificial Intelligence, and then providing the legal Writs that were necessary in Commissions to implement Restorative Justice this at a social level.

Through the Infiltration of the Archonic Souls Incarnated into the Human Bodies that Control the Media, the human race has been hypnotized into thinking that Medical "vaccinations", [which are not vaccinations] that they are getting is to cure some infection [which they are not]. These are Bio Weapons deployed to terminate Divine Souls.

And this is a component of the Lucifer Rebellion Rip in the Space Time Fabric Of The Organic Earth Timelines Zero going back from 1942 to 1744 with the first incursion of the 10,000 Archonic souls into Bavaria with the birth of the Bauers or the Rothschilds.

This is part of the Chronogarchy surveillance and expose that we at the Forward Time Base in 2045 have been sending up and down Earth's Organic Timeline from 1744 to 2522, the 500th anniversary of the publication of the Chronogarchy book.

When we've been able to vouch safe the Organic Divine Timeline Of Earth Zero safe from the Lucifer Rebellion all the way back through 1744, when there was that super attack from

1942 Third Reich, as 10,000 Archonic souls entered the Rip in Earth's Space Time Fabric.

Let's expose and identify some of Incarnations of the Archonic souls, right at 2020, just before the two Earth Timelines split at 2022. These are names that would be familiar to those along the timeline, that are tuned in to this timeline broadcast roughly at the time of the Separation of the Timelines — the year 2022.

When you tune in at 2020, you are tuned in at the time of Luciferian attack on Earth's Organic Timeline Known as the 2019-2020-2021+ Genocidal Technologies Pandemic.

So we're going to be reading off a series of names that actually are Indicted Incarnated, Archonic Reptilian, Luciferian Souls. At the Soul Incarnation Level, since the Rip of the Earth Organic Timeline, going back from 1942 to 1744, they're part of the swarm of 10,000 souls that have been dominating in politics, science, religion, and all of these control fields, oppressing humanity, and implementing the Lucifer Rebellion to exterminate Divine Human Souls on the planet and turn Earth into a Luciferian AI Artificial Intelligence Planet.

We're at 2045 Forward Time Base starting that now. We are reading from the Indictment that was set out by the Natural And Common Law Tribunal For Public Health And Justice that you can find online at www.Peaceinspace.org

We're reading from that Indictment now and, you can see and comprehend the True Meaning of that Indictment that now.

5G/COVID-19 Pandemic Perpetrator Defendants

Xi JinPing, General Secretary of the Communist Party, the Chairman of the Central Military Commission and Core Leader of Peoples Republic of China, and Executive over China Armed Forces, Intelligence Agencies, Bioweapons laboratories, Public Health Agencies, Vaccination, and COVID Social Control Policies

Vladimir Vladimirovich Putin, President of the Russian Federation and Executive over Russian Armed Forces, Intelligence Agencies, Bioweapons Laboratories, Public Health Agencies, Vaccination, and COVID Social Control Policies

Donald J. Trump, 45th President of the United States of America, and Executive over US Armed Forces, Intelligence Agencies, Bioweapons laboratories, Public Health Agencies, OPERATON WARP SPEED Vaccination, and COVID Social Control Policies

Joseph R. Biden, 46th President[-Elect] of the United States of America, and Executive over US Armed Forces, Intelligence Agencies, Bioweapons laboratories, Public Health Agencies, Vaccination, and COVID Social Control Policies

Benjamin Netanyahu, Prime Minister of Israel, Leader of Likud, and of Armed Forces, Intelligence Agencies, Bioweapons laboratories, Public Health Agencies, Vaccination, and COVID Social Control Policies

Boris Johnson, Prime Minister of the UK, Leader of the Conservative Party, and of the UK Armed Forces, Intelligence Agencies, Bioweapons laboratories, Public Health Agencies, Vaccination, and COVID Social Control Policies

Matt Hancock, UK Secretary of State for Health and Social Care, accountable for 5G rollout and COVID Genocidal Technologies Vaccinations and Social Control Policies

Elizabeth Alexandra Mary Windsor, Elizabeth II, Head of State of UK, and her consort, Philip Mountbatten, and their son Charles Windsor, Prince of Wales, individually and collectively

The Crown Corporation and any and all of its Subsidiaries including and not limited to Serco

Narendra Modi, Prime Minister of India, and Leader of the Indian Armed Forces, Intelligence Agencies, Bioweapons laboratories, Public Health Agencies, Vaccination, and COVID Social Control Policies

Emmanuel Jean-Michel Frédéric Macron, President of France, and Leader of the French Armed Forces, Intelligence Agencies, Bioweapons laboratories, Public Health Agencies, Vaccination, and COVID Social Control Policies and Edouard Phillipe, Prime Minister of France

Angela Merkel, Chancellor of Germany, Christian Democratic Party, and Leader of German Armed Forces, Intelligence Agencies, Bioweapons laboratories, Public Health Agencies, Vaccination, and COVID Social Control Policies

Justin Trudeau, Prime Minister of Canada, Leader of the Liberal Party, and of the Canadian Armed Forces, Intelligence Agencies, Bioweapons laboratories, Public Health Agencies, Vaccination, and COVID Social Control Policies

Scott Morrison, Prime Minister of Australia, Leader of the Liberal Party, and of the Australian Armed Forces, Intelligence Agencies, Bioweapons laboratories, Public Health Agencies, Vaccination, and COVID Social Control Policies

Jacinda Ardern, Prime Minister of New Zealand, Leader of the Labour Party, and of the New Zealand Armed Forces, Intelligence Agencies, Bioweapons laboratories, Public Health Agencies, Vaccination, and COVID Social Control Policies

António Guterres, Secretary General of the United Nations Organization, New York, New York, USA, Leader of UN Public Health Agencies, Vaccination, and COVID Social Control Policies

European Union, and President of the Commission, Ursula von der Leyen; President of the Parliament, David Sassoli; President of the European Council; Charles Michel; Presidency of the Council of the EU, Germany https://europa.eu

A 2009-2020 Lockstep Criminal Co-conspiracy, including and not limited to individually and collectively:

World Economic Forum, Klaus Schwab, and Officers, Directors, Employees, and Agents
Bill and Melinda Gates, Individually
Bill and Melinda Gates Foundation
Michael Bloomberg
David Rockefeller, Jr.
Warren Buffett
George Soros
Ted Turner
Oprah Winfrey
Rockefeller Foundation
Global Business Network [GBN]
Peter Schwartz, Chairman GBN, Individually
Other unknown and un-named co-conspirators and Defendants
World Health Organization [WHO] and Officers, Directors, Employees, and Agents
Tedros Adhanom Ghebreyesus, WHO Director General, Individually
Michael Ryan, WHO
CEO's at GCHQ-UK, NSA-USA and Bilderberg Group, all CEOs, Monarchies, and Members

Anthony Stephen Fauci, MD, Individually Bioweapons Laboratory, Fort Dietrich, MD, USA

Dr. Charles Lieber, 60, Chair of the Department of Chemistry and Chemical Biology at Harvard University

Yanqing Ye, 29, a Chinese national, Zaosong Zheng, 30, a Chinese national, was arrested on Dec. 10, 2019, at Boston's Logan International Airport and charged by criminal complaint with attempting to smuggle 21 vials of biological research to China.

International Olympic Committee, 2012 London International Olympics Event 201, Organizers and Attendees, October 18, 2019, New York, NY

World Military Games, Wuhan China, Organizing Committee and Attending National Delegations, October 18-27, 2019

The Wuhan BioSafety Lab-4 (BSL-4) and any and all BSL-4 labs in the United States, Europe, Russia, China, and Israel, which exist to create unlawfully biological warfare agents using DNA genetic engineering, and whose officers, directors, or employees violate the BioWeapons Act of 1989, and Article 6 and 7 of the International Criminal Code, including as part of Operation Lockstep 2010-2020, in criminal co-conspiracy with Defendant World Health Organization WHO.

Financial, Banking, and Pandemic Unjust Enrichment Defendants

International Monetary Fund and Managing Director Kristalina Georgieva
https://www.imf.org/external/index.htm

Bank for International Settlements, Member Central Banks, Board Chairman Jens Weidmann, Frankfurt am Main, Agustin Carstens, Manager
https://www.bis.org/

Federal Reserve Board, Member Banks of the 12 Federal Reserve Districts, and Chairman Jerome H. Powell
https://www.federalreserve.gov

Institute for the Works of Religion [Vatican Bank]
http://www.ior.va

Jesuits
https://www.jesuits.global

Any and All National Monetary Authorities, Money and Banking Regulators, Commercial Banks, Investment Banks specifically and intentionally financing Genocidal and Crimes Against Humanity activities associated with the 5G-Pandemic.

Major commercial banks including and not limited to: Lloyds, Barclays, HSBC, Nat West, Bank of Scotland, Deutsche bank, Danske Bank, and:

1 Industrial and Commercial Bank of China 4,324.27
2 China Construction Bank 3,653.11
3 Agricultural Bank of China 3,572.98
4 Bank of China 3,270.15
5 Mitsubishi UFJ Financial Group 2,892.97
6 HSBC 2,715.15
7 JPMorgan Chase 2,687.38
8 Bank of America 2,434.08
9 BNP Paribas 2,429.26
10 Crédit Agricole 2,256.72
11 Japan Post Bank 1,984.62
12 SMBC Group 1,954.78
13 Citigroup Inc. 1,951.16

(109) 7
14 Wells Fargo 1,927.26
15 Mizuho Financial Group 1,874.89
16 Banco Santander 1,702.61
17 Société Générale 1,522.05
18 Barclays 1,510.14
19 Groupe BPCE 1,501.59
20 Postal Savings Bank of China 1,467.31
21 Deutsche Bank 1,456.26
22 Bank of Communications 1,422.63
23 Royal Bank of Canada 1,116.31
24 Lloyds Banking Group 1,104.42
25 Toronto-Dominion Bank 1,102.04

26 China Merchants Bank 1,065.25

27 Intesa Sanpaolo 1,057.82

28 Norinchukin Bank 1,011.14

29 ING Group 1,000.72

30 Goldman Sachs 992.97

31 Industrial Bank (China) 976.79

32 Crédit Mutuel 976.14

33 UBS 972.18

34 UniCredit 960.21

35 China Minsheng Bank 959.63

36 NatWest Group 957.60

37 Shanghai Pudong Development Bank 950.01

38 China CITIC Bank 904.02

39 Morgan Stanley 895.43

40 Scotiabank 872.62

41 Credit Suisse 812.91

42 Banco Bilbao Vizcaya Argentaria 782.16

43 State Bank of India 730.54

44 Standard Chartered 720.40

45 Commonwealth Bank 688.40

46 China Everbright Bank 679.81

(109) 8

47 Bank of Montreal 665.20

48 Rabobank 662.77

49 Australia and New Zealand Banking Group 661.72

50 DZ Bank 627.31

51 Nordea 622.66

52 Westpac 611.47

53 National Australia Bank 571.34

54 Ping An Bank 565.72

55 Danske Bank 564.83

56 Resona Holdings 549.51

57 Sumitomo Mitsui Trust Holdings 509.28

58 Canadian Imperial Bank of Commerce 495.99

59 U.S. Bancorp 495.43

60 Sberbank of Russia 482.53

61 Shinhan Bank 478.50

62 Commerzbank 478.40

63 Truist Financial Corp 473.08

64 KB Financial Group Inc 449.15

65 CaixaBank 439.25

66 DBS Bank 430.45

67 Nomura Holdings 425.50

68 Huaxia Bank 422.74

69 ABN AMRO Group 420.89

70 PNC Financial Services 410.30

71 Itaú Unibanco 407.37

72 Capital One 390.37

73 The Bank of New York Mellon 381.51

74 Bank of Beijing 374.97

75 Nonghyup Bank 369.92

76 OCBC Bank 365.57

77 Banco do Brasil 365.51

78 Hana Financial Group 365.10

79 Banco Bradesco 345.21

(109) 9

80 China Guangfa Bank 343.26

81 Handelsbanken 328.59

82 KBC Bank 327.87

83 Caixa Econômica Federal 321.68

84 DNB ASA 317.75

85 Woori Bank 313.54

86 Nationwide Building Society 307.45

87 Bank of Shanghai 306.04

88 SEB Group 305.79

89 La Banque postale 304.88

90 United Overseas Bank 300.68

91 Bank of Jiangsu 296.58

92 Landesbank Baden-Württemberg 287.99
93 Erste Group 275.72
94 Industrial Bank of Korea 275.54
95 BayernLB 266.27
96 Qatar National Bank 259.48
97 China Zheshang Bank 258.63
98 Swedbank 257.79
99 Raiffeisen Gruppe 256.43
100 Banco Sabadell 251.10

Trillionaires & Billionaires for Unjust Enrichment
Quarantine that obliterated America's Middle class.
Jeff Bezos (Amazon)increase = $36.2 billion
Mark Zuckerberg (Facebook)increase = $30.1 billion
Elon Musk (Space X)increase = $14.1 billion
Sergey Steve Brin(Google)increase = $13.9 billion
Larry Page (Google)= $13.7 billion
Steve Ballmer (Microsoft)= $13.3 billion
MacKenzie Bezos (Amazon)= $12.6 billion
Michael Bloomberg (Bloomberg)= $12.1 billion
Bill Gates (Microsoft/BMGF)= $11.8 billion
Larry Ellison (Oracle)= $8.5 billion

(109) 10
Mark Zuckerberg — From March 18 to June 4 Zuckerberg increased his wealth 52% to over $83 billion, according to the report. CNBC

According to that report, the total net worth of America's billionaires rose 15% during the two months, from $2.9 trillion to $3.4 trillion. FORBES

Jeff Bezos, founder and CEO of Amazon, was the biggest winner as his fortune grew by $36.2 billion to $202 billion between March 18 and June 4, IPS said. BUSINESS INSIDER.

Mainstream Media/Social Media Disinformer Perpetrators of the 5G/Genocidal Technologies Pandemic — Defendants

Any beneficial Owners of and all online, print or other news media, television, radio, social media, video and audio platform, ISP, corporations, entities, individuals, editors, reporters, journalists, TV anchors, Operation Mockingbird clandestine officers, wherever located that has and continues to intentionally publish false information about, censor or delete from publication legitimate, science and journalistic-based information, constitutionally protected news, information and research regarding causal relationship of 5G/AI Coronavirus, Coronavirus Vaccinations, and Coronavirus Social Control Methods to the genocide and crimes against humanity that all human beings similarly situated are now in imminent danger of, including and not limited to:

Michael Bloomberg — Bloomberg LP and Bloomberg Media,
Rupert Murdoch — News Corp
Donald and Samuel "Si" Newhouse — Advance Publications
Cox Family — Atlanta Journal-Constitution
Jeff Bezos — The Washington Post
John Henry — The Boston Globe
Sheldon Adelson — The Las Vegas Review-Journal
Joe Mansueto — Inc. and Fast Company magazines
Mortimer Zuckerman — US News & World Report, New York Daily News
Barbey family — Village Voice
Stanley Hubbard — Hubbard Broadcasting
Patrick Soon-Shiong — Tribune Publishing Co.
Carlos Slim Helu — The New York Times
Warren Buffett — regional daily papers
Viktor Vekselberg — Gawker
Sumner Redstone — Viacom

CEO's at the Associated Press and TV Networks,
Richard Branson and all CEO's at Virgin Media, Virgin Health, and
CEO's at Virgin controlling all NHS (National Health Service Contracts)

CEO's Clarion group,
CEO's at BBC, ABC, STV, ITV, Granada TV, Grampion Tv, ABC,
Channel 4 and Channel 5
CEO's at UK Russell's Lawfirm,
CEO's at UK Charles Russell's Lawfirm, Russell's Group,
CEO's, Bindman and Partners,
CEO's at Ronald Fletcher and Co,
CEO's at Goodman Derrick,
CEO's at Economist Group associated Intel agencies and Publications,
CEO's at UBM,
CEO'S at CONPACT UK LTD,
Christopher Gossage, Tony/David English, Richard Hannah,
Dame Helen Alexander, James Manson, Tamsin Allen,
Jefferey Bindman, Derek Rosenblatt, Brian Nicholson
Reference: http://thefarrellreport.net

Time Warner

Home Box Office (HBO)
Time Inc.
CNN
Turner Broadcasting System, Inc.
Warner Bros. Entertainment Inc.
CW Network (partial ownership)
TMZ
New Line Cinema
Time Warner Cable
Cinemax
Cartoon Network
TBS
TNT
America Online (not majority shareholder)
MapQuest
Moviefone
Castle Rock

Sports Illustrated
Fortune
Marie Claire
People Magazine
Boomerang
Adult Swim
DC Comics

The Walt Disney Corporation

ABC Television Network
Disney Publishing
ESPN Inc.
Disney Channel
SOAPnet
A&E
Lifetime
NASCAR
Buena Vista Home Entertainment
Buena Vista Theatrical Productions

(109) 13
Buena Vista Records
Disney Records
Hollywood Records
Miramax Films
Touchstone Pictures
Walt Disney Pictures
Pixar Animation Studios
Buena Vista Games
Hyperion Books
Lucasfilm

Viacom

Paramount Pictures
Paramount Home Entertainment
Black Entertainment Television (BET)
Comedy Central
Country Music Television (CMT)
Logo
MTV
MTV Canada
MTV2
Nick Magazine
Nick at Nite
Nick Jr.
Nickelodeon
Noggin
Spike TV
The Movie Channel
TV Land
VH1
Epix
Atom Films
Viva
The Music Factory (TMF)

News Corporation

Dow Jones & Company, Inc.
Fox Television Stations
New York Post
Fox Searchlight Pictures
Beliefnet
Fox Business Network
Fox Kids Europe
Fox News Channel

(109) 14
Fox Sports Net
Fox Television Network
FX
My Network TV
MySpace
News Limited News
Phoenix InfoNews Channel
Phoenix Movies Channel
Sky PerfecTV
Speed Channel
STAR TV India
STAR TV Taiwan
STAR World
Times Higher Education Supplement Magazine
Times Literary Supplement Magazine
Times of London
20th Century Fox Home Entertainment
20th Century Fox International
20th Century Fox Studios
20th Century Fox Television
BSkyB
DIRECTV
Wall Street Journal
Fox Broadcasting Company
Fox Interactive Media
FOXTEL
HarperCollins Publishers
The National Geographic Channel
National Rugby League
News Corp Australia
News Interactive
News Outdoor
Radio Veronica
ReganBooks

Sky Italia
Sky Radio Denmark
Sky Radio Germany
Sky Radio Netherlands
STAR
The Sun
Sunday Times
Zondervan

CBS Corporation
CBS News

(109) 15
CBS Sports
CBS Television Network
CNET
Showtime
The Movie Channel
FLIX
TV.com
CBS Radio Inc. (130 stations)
CBS Consumer Products
CBS Outdoor
CW Network (50% ownership)
Infinity Broadcasting
Simon & Schuster (Pocket Books, Scribner)
Westwood One Radio Network
Last.fm
Charles Scribner's Sons
Pocket Books
Simon & Schuster

Comcast
NBC Universal
Bravo

CNBC
E! Entertainment
NBC News
MSNBC
NBC Sports
AT&T
NBC Television Network
Oxygen
SciFi Magazine
Syfy (Sci Fi Channel)
Telemundo
USA Network
Weather Channel
Focus Features
NBC Universal Television Distribution
NBC Universal Television Studio
Paxson Communications (partial ownership)
Trio
Universal Parks & Resorts
Universal Pictures
Universal Studio Home Video

CBC Canadian Broadcasting Corporation
BBC British Broadcasting Corporation

Social Media
Facebook Inc, A Delaware Corporation
Mark Eliot Zuckerberg, Individually
Twitter, Inc.
Google Inc., Alphabet, Inc.
You Tube
Vimeo

COVID Vaccinations:

Russian Federation, Rospotrebnadzor, COVID Vaccine Program
People's Republic of China, National Institutes for Food and Drug Control,
COVID Vaccine Program
United States of America, Operation Warp Speed, COVID Vaccine Program
World Health Organization COVAX, COVID Vaccine Program
Global Alliance Vaccine Initiative [GAVI], The Vaccine Alliance, including and not limited to its COVID Vaccine Program
Pope Francis I, nee Jorge Mario Bergoglio, the bishop of Rome, the head of the Catholic Church and sovereign of the Vatican City State, and the first Jesuit pope.

COVID Vaccinations &
any and all Vaccinations

Arcturus Therapeutics (NASDAQ:ARCT) $249.1 million
BioNTech (NASDAQ:BNTX) $12.2 billion
CSL Behring (OTC:CSLL.Y) $89.8 billion
Dynavax (NASDAQ:DVAX) $293.9 million
GlaxoSmithKline (NYSE:GSK) $93.7 billion
Inovio Pharmaceuticals (NASDAQ:INO) $1.2 billion
Johnson & Johnson (NYSE:JNJ) $357.9 billion
Moderna (NASDAQ:MRNA) $11.4 billion
Novavax (NASDAQ:NVAX) $821.8 million
Pfizer (NYSE:PFE) $190.2 billion
Sanofi (NASDAQ:SNY) $112.9 billion
TranslateBio (NASDAQ:TBI

Testing:

Abbott Labs (NYSE:ABT) $142 billion
Bayer $60.2 billion
Becton Dickinson (NYSE:BDX) $63.2 billion

bioMerieux (OTC:BMXMF) $13.2 billion
Co-Diagnostics (NASDAQ:CODX) $273 million
Danaher (NYSE:DHR) $98.5 billion
Eli Lilly $135.8 billion
Grifols $19.5 billion
LabCorp (NYSE:LH) $11.9 billion
OPKO Health (NASDAQ:OPK) $817.2 million
Quest Diagnostics (NYSE:DGX) $10.4 billion

(109) 23
Roche Holdings $286.7 billion
Thermo Fisher Scientific (NYSE:TMO) $117.7 billion

Vaccinations
Imperial College London UK for manufacture and distribution of vaccines called Vaccine 1 AMBUSH Vaccine 2 TRIUMPH

Pharmaceutical companies working on COVID 19 Vaccines and any and all Vaccinations[By website]:

G4S
https://www.g4s.com

Serco
https://www.serco.com

Imperial College London for manufacture and distribution of Vaccine 1 AMBUSH Vaccine 2 TRIUMPH
https://www.imperial.ac.uk/

AstraZeneca — For COVID 19 Vaccines and for any and all Vaccinations
https://www.astrazeneca.com/

Merck & Co. — For Gardasil, and for any and all Vaccinations
https://www.merck.com/

Pfizer — For COVID 19 Vaccines and for any and all Vaccinations
https://www.pfizer.com/

The Pirbright Institute
https://www.pirbright.ac.uk/

For COVID 19 Vaccines and for any and all Vaccinations:

https://twistbioscience.com/
http://www.gsk.com/
https://www.distributedbio.com/
http://www.pluristem.com/

(109) 24
https://www.janssen.com/
https://www.modernatx.com/
http://sorrentotherapeutics.com/
https://www.flowpharma.com/
https://www.flowpharma.com/
http://medicago.com/
https://www.inovio.com/
https://www.centivax.com/
https://www.abcellera.com/
https://vaccitech.co.uk/
http://www.curevac.com/
https://zyduscadila.com/
https://immunoprecise.com/
http://www.ligandal.com/
http://www.emergentbiosolutions.com/
http://www.cansinotech.com/
https://www.vir.bio/
http://www.sanofipasteur.com/
https://biocadglobal.com/
https://smartpharmtx.com/
https://www.helixnano.com/
codagenix.com

adaptivebiotech.com

(109) 25
generex.com
swiftscalebio.com
vaxess.com
heatbio.com
houstonmethodist.org
synairgen.com
dynavax.com
themisbio.com
epivax.com
altimmune.com
vaxart.com
cloverbiopharma.com
geovax.com
novavax.com
univercells.com
sinovac.com
allovir.com
biontech.de
tonixpharma.com
ipharminc.com
halovax.com
immunomix.com
diosvax.com

(109) 26
kiadis.com
southernresearch.org
ajvaccines.com,
niaid.nih.gov/
idtdna.com,
bravovax.com

Wuhan Vaccine
kernalbio.com
arcturusrx.com
genscript.com
diadembio.com
cc-pharming.com

Beijing Vaxine
vaxine.net
vido.org
genels.com

Seoul
voltrontx.com
advaccine.com

China
Beijing
vaxine.net

Aspartame — Genocide and Crimes against Humanity by Any and all uses of Aspartame by any name in any formulation in any product for human consumption including and not limited to Vaccinations

Defendant Donald H. Rumsfeld, Developer of Aspartame and Convicted War Criminal, Kuala Lumpur War Crimes Tribunal 2011-12

Official Communications Regulators of All Nations Approving Roll-out of 5G and 60GHz transmission systems

Federal Communications Commission FCC, USA
OFCOM UK https://www.ofcom.org.uk/
International Commission on Non-Ionizing Radiation Protection
International Telecommunications Union (ITU)
US Department of Defense (DOD)
DARPA

(109) 28

Serco Group

Crown Castle

British Nuclear Fuels (BNFL)

British Atomic Weapons Establishment (AWE)

Neuralink

CERN

Central Intelligence Agency (CIA)

National Security Agency (NSA)

NASA

US Air Force

US Navy

CERN

O2

Center for Strategic and International Studies (CSIS)

Strategic Communications Laboratories (SCL)

World Health Organization WHO

Ministry of Health, Chinese Center for Disease Control and Prevention,

People's Republic of China

Rospotrebnadzor, Health Authority, Russian Federation,

CDC Centers for Disease Control, USA

National Health Service, UK

The National Institute for Health and Care Excellence

https://www.nice.org.uk/

The UK Nursing and Midwifery Council

https://www.nmc.org.uk/

The General Medical Council

https://www.gmc-uk.org/

The Health and Care Professions Council

https://www.hcpc-uk.org/

The UK Medicines and Healthcare Products Regulatory Agency
https://www.gov.uk/government/organisations/medicines-and-healthcare-products-regulatory-agency

Health Canada

Public Health Authorities for all Member states of the United Nations Organization.

Provincial and State Health Authorities for all Member states of the

SUMMARY OF PROBABLE CAUSE EVIDENCE IN INDICTMENT

Probable Cause Evidence of Irreparable Harm to all Human Beings similarly situated, in violation of Articles 6 and 7 of the International Criminal Code

I. 5G/AI Coronavirus Genocide — Probable Cause Evidence of Irreparable Harm to all human beings similarly situated, in violation of Articles 6 and 7 of the International Criminal Code

II. AI/Coronavirus/COVID-19 Vaccinations-related Genocide, which must be stopped. – Probable Cause Evidence of Irreparable Harm to all human beings similarly situated, in violation of Articles 6 and 7 of the International Criminal Code

III. 5G AI/Coronavirus Social Control Methods Genocide — Probable Cause Evidence of Irreparable Harm to all human beings similarly situated, in violation of Articles 6 and 7 of the International Criminal Code

Therefore, the probable cause evidence submitted above demonstrates beyond any reasonable doubt that the 5G AI/Coronavirus Social Control Methods Genocide of Defendants named and unnamed is causing imminent and Irreparable Harm to all human beings similarly situated, in violation of Articles 6 and 7 of the

103

International Criminal Code and must be stopped by this Court with a Writ of Emergency Injunction.

IV. Defendants known and unknown continue in criminal conspiracy to create 5G/AI-Coronavirus Genocide as clandestinely developed and carried out carried out in Rockefeller Foundation/Global Business Report Lockstep 2010, London Olympics Opening Ceremony & Games, July 27-August 12, 2012, Event 201 October 18, 2019 (New York), World Military Games October 18-27, 2019 (Wuhan China), and numerous 5G/AI wifi-technology and Coronavirus approving, manufacturing, and distribution and sales entities, corporations, and individuals thereby causing irreparable harm to all human beings similarly situated in violation of Articles 6 and 7 or the International Criminal Code.

V. Role of Inorganic Sentient and Strong AI Artificial Intelligence in 5G/AI-Coronavirus Genocide and Crimes Against humanity

Emergency Relief Requested

1. 5G/AI-Coronavirus Genocide Emergency Relief —
A Writ of Emergency Injunction

2. Any and all Vaccinations and Coronavirus or COVID-19 related Vaccination Genocide: Emergency Relief — A Writ of Emergency Injunction

3. Coronavirus Social Control Methods Genocide: Emergency Relief Requested — A Writ of Emergency Injunction

4. Freedom of Information Emergency Relief — A Writ of Emergency Injunction

5. Equitable Relief Requested: Writ of Mandamus and Restorative Justice
Restorative Justice vs Retributive Justice:
Tribunal: an Equitable Writ of Mandamus

(1) Defendants' Unjust Enrichment: Tribunal: an Equitable Writ of Mandamus

(2) 5G/AI Coronavirus Genocide Truth and Reconciliation Commission:

October 13, 2010 Overflight Of Regional Galactic Governance Council's Federation Fleet Over Manhattan New York City As Predicted By Federation To NORAD OFFICER Stanley A. Fulham And Reported Worldwide By Zofyo Arni, Whose Decade Of Contact Inaugurated Council's Overt Intervention In 2000

UN Outer Space Office & Conference
Decade of Contact
Regional Galactic Governance Council
Stanley A Fulham

2010 NARRATION: October 13th, 2010 overflight of Regional Galactic Governance Council Federation Fleet over Manhattan, New York City, as predicted by the Federation to lifelong NORAD officer Stanley A. Fulham and as reported worldwide by Zofyo Arni in interviews with Stanley A. Fulham. The Regional Galactic Governance Council is Universe Governance, Upper Dimensional Human Federation that has been overseeing the affairs of life-bearing planet Earth on Earth Organic Timeline Zero for the last 1 million years.

The original Galactic Governance Council membership includes contiguous upper dimensional human civilizations, including the Pleiades

Orion
Sirius
Bootes
Alpha Centauri
Comsuli
Zeta Reticuli
Pouseti.

In January, 2010, the Regional Galactic Governance Council had met in extraordinary session and had decided that the environmental degradation of Earth's ecology was such that it required immediate overt intervention by the Federation's technology to keep the Earth's environmental ecology from collapsing.

This is one of the few instances over the last million years where the Regional Galactic Governance Council has decided to intervene overtly in the affairs of any planet, let alone make themselves known on that planet. The Regional Galactic Governance Council by its own terms in its communications with lifelong NORAD officer Stanley A. Fulham, whose job it was while a NORAD to dispatch jet interceptors at any incursion over North America by UFO's unidentified spaceships.

They let Stanley A. Fulham know that their desire, the desire of the Regional Galactic Governance Council was to intervene at the United Nations in New York. As it so happened, the date the Council chose for initial UN intervention was on October 14th, 2010, the day after the overflight of the Fleet of the Galactic Governance Council on October 13th, 2010.

The United Nations Outer Space Office, which normally met in Vienna, Austria, was scheduled to meet on October 14,

2010 at UN headquarters in New York to discuss UN protocols for welcoming a delegation of Intelligent Civilizations from the Universe, ie Extraterrestrials.

It was in this context and this backdrop that on October 13th, 2010, the Spaceship Fleet of the Regional Galactic Governance Council showed itself over New York's Manhattan, with the context and the message of the Regional Galactic Council.

This Regional Galactic Council showing itself had already been published that previous summer in June of 2010.

Former NORAD officer Stanley A Fulham released his book, the Challenge Of Change in which there was reprinted the substantive communications that he had with the Council of 8 on behalf of the Regional Galactic Governance Council,.

Through their Representatives that had met with Stanley A Fulham Interdimensionally *in persona*, in which it was explained to him who exactly the Regional Galactic Governance Council was, what their mission was of Oversight over planet Earth and its contiguous life-bearing planets for the last million years. And, their concern that the Environment of Earth was deteriorating to such an extent that the Ecology of Earth might collapse. Such a collapse would be jeopardizing Earth as an Intelligent Life-Bearing Human Planet requiring, for the first time in living memory and overt intervention of the Regional Galactic Governments Council with its advanced technology to repair and permanently fix the Ecology of the Earth.

How was the Earth Ecology in peril you might ask? Well, that's very simple. With the attacks on the Earth and the Earth Ecology by the combined forces of an Invading Sentient Pathogenic, Predatory Artificial Intelligence, the Draco Reptilians, the Orion Gray's going back to via the Third Reich in1942, created a Rip in the Time Space Fabric Of Earth, going back to 1744. This allowed a swarm of Archonic souls, starting in 1744 to enter into Earth's Incarnation Platform.

These 10,000 Archonic souls begin a secret plan of displacing Human Souls and incarnating into all positions of power with a secret destructive plan in Government Leadership, Monarchies, Finances, Religions, Media, Science, Military. They implemented a planetary policy of War, Disease, Crime, Poverty, And Environmental Degradation on planet Earth to terminate Earth as a Divine Human Soul Incarnation Venue. Their intent was to make Earth a Trans Humanist Agenda, AI Artificial Intelligence, Soul Planet, and that plan had taken its toll by the time the industrial revolution came. All of the issues of Environmental pollution had flourished on Earth through the 20th century, and the Oceans of the Earth were entirely polluted.

The Atmosphere of the Earth had been entirely polluted by nuclear testing, by industrial pollution, polluted urban cities, polluted air and waters of the earth, and, the Earth, even though still on Organic Timeline Zero, the foremost separation would not come until 2022 was, on the brink of collapse.

And that's what brought about what we're witnessing today. the Overflight Of The Regional Galactic Governance Council over Manhattan. and as we look up, we who are on the ground can see the ET Ships clearly in the air.

There are photographs of crowds along various avenues in Manhattan, looking up the to the Sky to see. And it's very clear for those Who Have Eyes To See And Ears To Hear That There Are Extraterrestrial Craft over Manhattan. For those who were tuned into the mission and who accessed and read NORAD officer Stanley Fulham's book, published in June of 2010 — they knew exactly what these visible objects were.

The Regional Galactic Governance Council, the Pleiadeans, the Alpha Centaurians, the Sirians, and others who were signaling their intention to land at the UN and signaling to the UN officials from the UN Outer Space Office and the others who were there for the Annual General Assembly Meeting, that the next day, October 14th, 2010, was an extremely important day. The UN Outer Space Office would be rolling out the Protocols For The Nations Of Earth and for the UN to welcome in effect the Regional Galactic Governance Council.

At this level of galactic reporting, even with planets like earth, which the Regional Galactic Governance Council has had to put in the column of Default Planets because of the Lucifer Rebellion, there was an unexpected rebellion of the Spiritual Dimension Oversight Senior Angelic Overseers For Planet Earth — Lucifer, Satan, and Caligastia — for the planets of this solar system.

The planets of the Solar System had been subjected to intense and destructive nuclear wars with a giant human planet Tiamat, 750,000 years before the October 13, 2010 Overflight approximately having been reduced to the Asteroid Belt. Another human life-bearing planet Mars was reduced in the war to a pumpkin-shaped planet, and its remaining 1 million inhabitants forced underground.

There were two planets at play, one being Venus, which was an Advanced Planet, that was in effect an Inside the Solar System Contact of the Regional Galactic Governance Council.

In that status, Venus was representing and holding the policy of the Regional Galactic Council inside the Solar System, because as the Advanced Extraterrestrial Civilization inside the Sol Solar System, Venus was in very active Liaison with The Regional Galactic Governance Council of the Pleiadeans, Alphas Centaurians, and Sirians and others. Venus was sort of the local Liaison planet and was sending Ambassadors To Earth, to stabilize Earth's Galactic status. For example, the Venusians sent an Ambassador to Earth during the Administration Of US President Eisenhower, who stayed at the Pentagon. Valiant Thor was an ambassador of the Venusians ambassador to the Pentagon on behalf of the Regional Galactic Governance Council.

And at the time of the Incarnation Of The Paradise Son of God, Jesus of Nazareth, other Venusian incarnates, accompanied Jesus as part of his Apostles, they were Venusians some of his apostles and disciples.

It has been said in speculation that Jesus himself was a Venusian incarnate. However, that is not the case. Jesus did not have a Venusian incarnation. Jesus Divine Soul actually came through the Hunab Ku, galactic black hole at the center of the Milky way galaxy. That's the portal to the central most place of Uversa of Spiritual Dimensions paradise of realms of our universe.

And that's just, you know, you may think it's Inside Baseball, but it's just to keep these things technical and technically correct. Well, back to October 13th, 2010, this is a very unusual event. And, it's a day that, during which, the Regional Galactic Governance Council made its presence known and its mandate to intervene in the United Nations, so that the technology, the environmental technology, their Advanced Environmental Technology could cure the world.

We are fortunate that the journalist, Zofyo Arni, reported on that day, and we have his reports, which are a record from that day.

We're also are fortunate to have a Reporter on the ground, from that day October 13th, 2010, Sappho Sherman, who was on the ground, in Manhattan, in the vicinity of 42nd street, along the East river, along the United Nations building.

And, we're going to ask her, watch her, what her experience was, Sappho.

Sappho can you come through and share what is your experience? You see crowds? Are other people on the ground actually experiencing and identifying the craft of the Regional Galactic Governance Council that are in the skies?

REPORTER SAPPHO SHERMAN: Thank you very much for, for contacting us. You know, I, I've got to tell you that News York City is a hard-boiled city. And as you may recall, the Regional Galactic Governance Council in its conversations with NORAD officer Stanley A. Fulham, as he reports it, chose New York to manifest the Fleet because, New Yorkers are very, hard boiled feet on the ground.

They're kind of, hard-boiled, especially at this 2010 kind of era. I'm here at, the 42nd Street and East River Location right now, adjacent to the grounds of the United Nations Building.

And we're looking up at the sky and yes, we have up there, the Fleet of the Regional Galactic Governance Council. And I can tell you that, the sidewalks are, the people on the sidewalks who are cognizant of this. and I would say it would be about maybe 30 to 40% of the people that are here, are looking up at the skies and really understanding what's going on.

There's another 30% of the people here. So about 60 to 70% of the people are looking up at the other 30% are looking out and, wondering what's that what's that because they aren't tuned into, what we could call the Exopolitical landing of the Regional Galactic Governance Council, even though the Regional Galactic Governance Council gave full warning to the lifelong NORAD officer, Stanley A. Fulham.

And this is a very exciting day. We can see the ET craft; their outline is quite full. The craft are of the Pleiadean type that are easily recognizable, that have been identified. Interstellar craft that have been identified on missions from the Pleiades to the Earth's Solar System, as well as, on missions from Sirius and missions from Alpha Centauri.

We are very, very, confident here that this is the mission as reported. And, as you state later in your report, you're going to be making available, one of the enduring reports by Zofyo Arni who is the Exopolitics reporter for the planet. Zofyo Arni has made official reports here in the Examiner newspaper as the Seattle Examiner, and who has been in touch with Stanley A. Fulham, who is in liaison with the Regional Galactic Governance Council.

In February of 1973, Zofyo Arni, future President Jimmy Carter and US Chrononaut Alexander Uine were contacted by the Regional Galactic Governance Council and taken aboard their ships. Planetary humans, including, President Jimmy Carter, Zofyo Arni, US Chrononaut Alexander Uine, have been contacted by the Regional Galactic Governance Council.

And now, the United Nations Outer Space Office that has a scheduled meeting on October 14th, 2010 has been contacted by that Regional Galactic Governance Council, as it rolls out its protocols, the engagement with extraterrestrials in this case, the elected governance council that has been responsible for the governance of Earth.

We have here a very well-prepared coherent contiguous event, a Galactic Governance Event. The Regional Galactic Governance Council has made clear that the purpose of its visit, following its unprecedented meeting, is that it needs to intervene to vouch safe the environment of the Earth before that collapses.

The Earth's environment has been in collapse because of the sustained pressure on it because of the, occupation of leadership positions by the Archonic souls that were able to make its way in during the Lucifer rebellion occupation.

What I'd like to do for you and for your listeners is to give a bit of a more context to this October 13th, 2010 Spaceship Fleet Overflight.

This fits within the framework of the new science of Exopolitics that appeared first on Earth in 2000 through the publication of Zofyo's book, Exopolitics, as a free eBook or the Internet in the year 2000. The 2005 softcover Exopolitics book had been Time Traveled back, to the Project Pegasus White Hats, back to 1971.

What the Exopolitics book introduced was a whole concept of a Decade Of Contact and acknowledged that Earth had been placed under a Quarantine. And it had been placed under a Quarantine by the Regional Galactic Governance Council on behalf of the Universe Administration, after it went into default because of the Lucifer Rebellion.

There needed to be a formal set of steps that needed to be taken, to bring the Earth back into a regular contact in the development of an intelligent life-bearing planet that Earth had lost out on because of the Lucifer Rebellion that had occurred here.

And so with Zofyo Arni's Exopolitics book that appeared in the year 2000 and as a soft cover in 2005 came the Decade Of Contact.

The concept of the Decade Of Contact, was that with Planet Earth, there would be a formal Decade taken in which there would be a great deal of attention paid to Extraterrestrial issues, to school the planet in Extraterrestrial issues.

And so with the publication of Zofyo Arni's Exopolitics book in the year 2000 then the Decade Of Contact initiated. The Regional Galactic Governance Council approved and took joint action on 10 years later, as part of the Decade Of Contact was the Regional Galactic Governance Council Overflight over in New York on October 13th, 2010.

You are now witnessing the fulfillment of the Decade Of Contact Proposal Prophecy as, first published in the year 2000 through the book, Exopolitics: A Decade of Contact Zofyo Arni, which was then undertaken and supported and approved by the Regional Galactic Governance Council starting in the year 2000.

Then, through all those subsequent years was internalized, in covert policy meetings here on Earth, with various governments and various proposals, and at the Regional Governance Council Level was communicated to NORAD officer Stanley A. Fulham, which then in the combination of the Decade Of Contact on October 13th, 2010, 10 years later resulted in the Overflight over, the United Nations and in effect the Landing Of The Regional Galactic Governance Council, which was acknowledged and recognized at all governmental levels, even though the community of reptilian and Archonic souls that control certain levels of the media, certain levels of governance and finance, sought to hide it out.

So that has been the business on this planet since 1744, as we know, through 1942, which is when the Third Reich Luciferians initiated the Rip across Earth's Space-Time back to 1744., the 10,000 incarnating souls came in, and that sort of Luciferian rebellion, a war at the soul level has been fought, so that the Environment Of Earth was really secured and made safe as of October 13th, 2010, when the technology of the Regional Galactic Governance Council was deployed throughout the environment and stabilized the Ecology Of Earth.

What we're going to do now is a few things to bring your audience up to date. We're going to leave you with an outline

---

of number one, the Decade Of Contact, which was published in the year 2000, and which was initiated in the year 2000 with the publication, a free eBook form of Exopolitics: A Decade of Contact, which the Original Galactic Governance Council then adopted as its formal policy toward, Planet Earth.

We're going to leave you with that incidentally, this was part of a futurist Zofyo Arni's own initiative in which he put himself forward as Earth Representative to the Regional Galactic Governance Council. And that was based upon his Proposed Decade Of Contact, first published in, the year 2000 as part of the Exopolitics book, which was then adopted by the Regional Galactic Governance Council, which then they implemented the Decade Of Contact in the decade from 2000 to October 13th, 2010, which is when they overflew the United Nations.

And on that day began the Restoration Using Advanced Galactic Technology to restore and stabilize the Environment of Earth. This was how Zofyo Arni's Proposal to be Earth's Representative To The Regional Galactic Governance Council was in fact accepted and implemented by the Regional Galactic Governance Council.

You can find that at www.positivefuture.info. We're going to leave you first with the contact proposal, which was 2000 to 2010, October 13th, 2010. And then, we are going to leave you with the United Nations Outer Space Conference, The Regional Galactic Governance Council, the report that Zofyo did on the October 13th, 2010 overflight.

You'll get the two Bookends from the year 2000 with a Decade Of Contact that kicked that off. And then, you'll get the October 13th, 2010 Regional Galactic Governance Council Overflight report.

That way, you will get the benefit of what we've been able to develop and what has been developed right before the eyes of those divine Soul-oriented Earthlings on Earth's Organic Timeline Zero, the Divine Oriented Timeline that at all times was appreciative and knew that Earth was firmly anchored into the Universe Administration as, coming down from the Spiritual

Dimensions, through Paradise, through the Incarnated Paradise Son through into this Universe Uversa, the Galactic Governance Council of the Pleiadeans, Sirians, Alpha Centaurians, and others.

And continued through Planet Earth, starting with the Decade Of Contact in the year 2000, and culminating in October 13th, 2010 with the Original Galactic Governance Council, accepting the proposal of the Representative Of Earth Zofyo Arni on the Zofyo Arni at that point, stabilizing the Environment Of Earth.

This is a Revelation that I, Sappho Sherman, am today, very happy to bring you. So, thank you very much. And, I now will take your questions. Thank you.

Exopolitics: A Decade of Contact

By Zofyo Arni
https://www.bibliotecapleyades.net/exopolitica/exopol/exopolitics04.htm#17
Year 2000

Chapter Seventeen
Toward A Decade of Contact

Fear should no longer paralyze us from seeking our membership in Universe society. One version of this fear, promoted by a military-intelligence network, is that we should fear an "invasion" of hostile aliens more than anything else.

Contemporary world leaders have said that such a hostile invasion would truly bring humankind together. Former United States Presidents have broadcast this message to the world in the 1980s at the United Nations, and as recently as late 1999. In a way, this "alien invasion" is the equivalent of the "Earth is the center of the Universe" message of the Middle Ages.

The "alien invasion" is a psychological war initiative, one more way that the vested interests of powerful terrestrial governments keep the human population isolated from the advances of interplanetary civilization.

What will bring humankind together is our accessing interplanetary government. There is no authentic "alien invasion" planned. That is disinformation. Universe government is advanced, organized, peaceful, and interested in our evolution. If there is any "rogue" extraterrestrial presence on Earth, it operates outside the confines of Universe laws and will end.

How can the human population get beyond the anti-extraterrestrial conceptual traps that our institutions and terrestrial leaders keep constructing for us? One way is to build a new, participatory exopolitical process whose purpose is to foment and structure humankind's preparedness to enter interplanetary society. Exopolitics will deconstruct negative disinformation about an extraterrestrial presence. Open research will shed the light of truth on alleged extraterrestrial plots to genetically enslave mankind.

The Decade of Contact is a ten-year participatory education-based process to facilitate integration with Universe society. We dedicate a ten-year period of education and community action around integrating Earth into Universe society. The Decade of Contact is both a process and a public attitude. Extraterrestrial contact is our doorway into re-integration with Universe society. Extraterrestrial contact is an interactive process; it involves mutual interaction between our fellow humans and Universe society. Just how many decades it will take to re-establish working contact with the organized Universe is partially in our own hands.

The Decade of Contact is simple and straightforward. Any individual, group, institution, nation, or government can participate. Participants in the Decade of Contact will commit to transform their lives, their institutional focus, and resources to re-establishing integration with organized interplanetary society. Rejoining Universe society is an exopolitical process, and will happen only as political momentum gathers at the personal, local, regional, and global levels. The process of Universe integration may take time in lift-off, like a space vehicle starting its long journey with slow lift-off from Earth.

Mobilizing the human species to integrate with Universe society will take place in many concurrent ways. A key task is the gathering of information, research, and scientific and educational resources about Universe society. Our dominant terrestrial model of reality is functionally a legacy from the Middle Ages. Our collective new knowledge base must be assembled from an exopolitical context.

There are also important cultural components to the Decade of Contact, as human awareness builds to a critical mass. These will include political movements, public events, concerts, music, art, and media to celebrate Universe society. Our reunion with Universe society is a ground of our basic human rights. The Decade of Contact process will transform our civilization from within, from a terrestrial culture to a Universal one.

Transformation of human society will occur when we reach a Universe-sensitive critical mass. With approximately forty-five percent of Earth's population now extraterrestrial-conscious, can critical mass be far behind?

ET Council: "We will Increase UFOs, Address UN in 2014, Renew Ecology in 2015

by Zofyo Arni

Seattle Exopolitics Examiner

October 23, 2010

from Examiner Website
https://www.bibliotecapleyades.net/vida_alien/alien_galacticfederations13.htm

Former NORAD officer Stanley A. Fulham

Photo: Stanley A. Fulham

In an exclusive, in-depth interview on Exopolitics Radio with Zofyo Arni, former NORAD officer Stanley A. Fulham has stated that a regional galactic governance authority, (the 'Council of 8') made a dramatic decision in January, 2010 to put aside the law of non-intervention.

At a solemn meeting, the 'Council of 8' decided to intervene with their technology to clean Earth's atmosphere before an environmental collapse occurs on Earth, as has happened on many other inhabited planets with civilizations similar to our own.

The 'Council of 8' did so, according to Mr. Fulham's information, after reaching a conclusion that that our human technology could not now prevent an environmental collapse and species extinction on Earth from occurring.

According to Mr. Fulham, this is a rare decision by the 'Council of 8', and is partly a result of Council members wishing to preserve the unique positive qualities of our human population.

The "Council of 8", according to Mr. Fulham's information, consists of the intelligent civilizations of, the Pleiades

Orion
Sirius
Bootes
Alpha Centauri
Comsuli
Zeta Reticuli
Pouseti

This cleanup of the Earth's atmosphere will, according to Mr. Fulham's information, commence in 2015 after a 2014 speech at the United Nations by the 'Council of 8''s Pleiadian representatives.

The 'Council of 8's' appearance in 2014 at the United Nation's General Assembly may occur, according to Mr. Fulham's information, following a collapse of the present world order and the emergence of a new way of living during the period 2010 – 2014.

This transitional 2010-14 period may be accompanied by possible earth changes, monetary collapse, and governmental and nation state collapse.

Mr. Fulham stated in his Exopolitics Radio interview that the regional galactic governance council ("Council of 8") had chosen

New York City for an initial Oct 13, 2010 UFO 'decloaking' because it was a global, cosmopolitan city with a blasé population that would not be frightened of their appearance.

There are multiple, independent evidentiary sources that prove the Oct. 13, 2010 UFO sightings over New York City were the result of an intervention by a non-Earthly intelligent civilization, and not the result of 'other causes' such as released balloons.

The original plan of the 'Council of 8', taken at a meeting in January 2010, had been for simultaneous UFO appearances on Oct 13, 2010 over major world cities.

The purpose of these 'Council of 8' UFO appearances, which are set to increase in the future, is to acclimatize Earth humans to the Council of 8's presence and decision to intervene.

The increased UFO sightings in the future are meant to lead up to a world speech by the 'Pleiadian' representatives of the 'Council of 8' in the General Assembly hall at the United Nations in 2014.

Examiner readers can listen to this in-depth historic interview with Stanley A. Fulham far below.

The 'Council of 8'

According to Mr. Fulham, the 'Council of 8' has had a caretaker role for our planet for about the last million years, and has effectively maintained Earth under protective quarantine following an attempted invasion and takeover of Earth.

Mr. Fulham has authored a book, Challenges of Change, containing the results of his 10 years investigation of the role of the 'Council of 8' and other entities in our galaxy and Universes.

Mr. Fulham writes that he obtained this information about the 'Council of 8' through an inter-dimensional intelligent civilization that monitors events in our galaxy and Universes.

Other experts such as Dr. Carl Johan Calleman have independently predicted in interviews with Zofyo Arni an end to hierarchies and the value of money, and increased extraterrestrial and UFO contact in the 2010-14 period.

On Oct. 14, 2010 — a day after the New York City UFO sightings — Dr. Mazian Othman, director of the U.N. Outer Space Office, delivered a wide-ranging 28-minute video press conference at the United Nations in New York during which she stated that 'ET life is a possibility' and remarked that the United Nations must ready itself for ET contact.

Historic 90-minute interview with Stanley A. Fulham on the 'Council of 8': ET contact, and ET environmental intervention

Examiner readers can listen to this historic 90-minute interview with Stanley A. Fulham and Zofyo Arni on the 'Council of 8', ET contact, and ET environmental intervention in 2015 by clicking below:

**Regional Galactic Governance Council (Council of 8):
ET contact, and ET environmental intervention-Historic
90-minute interview with NORAD Officer Stanley A. Fulham**

https://newsinsideout.com/2019/11/historic-90-minute-interview-with-norad-officer-stanley-a-fulham-on-the-regional-galactic-governance-council-council-of-8-et-contact-and-et-environmental-intervention/

November 10, 2019 By Zofyo Arni 7 Comments

NORAD Officer Stanley A. Fulham: Regional Galactic Governance Council

Readers can now listen to this historic 90-minute interview with Stanley A. Fulham and Zofyo Arni on the Regional Galactic Governance Council (Council of 8), ET contact, and ET environmental intervention:

LISTEN TO INTERVIEW ON TRUETUBE.CO
https://youtu.be/r3pwSJ0EKvU

Fulham, Stanley A., Challenges of Change (2010)
https://www.amazon.com/Challenges-Change-Stanley-Fulham-ebook/dp/B0080BWQBW

VANCOUVER, BC — In an exclusive, in-depth interview on Exopolitics Radio with Zofyo Arni, former NORAD officer

Stanley A. Fulham has stated that a regional galactic governance authority, (the 'Council of 8') made a dramatic decision in January, 2010 to put aside the law of non-intervention.

At a solemn meeting, the Regional Galactic Governance Council (Council of 8) decided to intervene with their technology to clean Earth's atmosphere before an environmental collapse occurs on Earth, as has happened on many other inhabited planets with civilizations similar to our own.

The Regional Galactic Governance Council (Council of 8) did so, according to Mr. Fulham's information, after reaching a conclusion that that our human technology could not now prevent an environmental collapse and species extinction on Earth from occurring.

According to Mr. Fulham, this is a rare decision by the Regional Galactic Governance Council (Council of 8), and is partly a result of Council members wishing to preserve the unique positive qualities of our human population.

Regional Galactic Governance Council (Council of 8)

The Regional Galactic Governance Council (Council of 8), according to Mr. Fulham's information, consists of the intelligent civilizations of the Pleiades, Orion, Sirius, Bootes, Alpha Centauri, Comsuli, Zeta Reticuli, and Pouseti. [Ed. Note: A preliminary search failed to reveal a known star system or constellation named 'Comsuli or 'Pouseti'.]

This cleanup of the Earth's atmosphere will, according to Mr. Fulham's information, commence after a speech at the United Nations by the Regional Galactic Governance Council (Council of 8)'s Pleiadian representatives.

The Regional Galactic Governance Council (Council of 8)'s appearance at the United Nation's General Assembly may occur, according to Mr. Fulham's information, following a collapse of the present world order and the emergence of a new way of living during the period.

Possible earth changes, monetary collapse, and governmental and nation state collapse

This transitional period may be accompanied by possible earth changes, monetary collapse, and governmental and nation state collapse. Stanley A. Fulham originally identified the transitional period as being 2010-15. However, given both the non-linear and non-temporal interdimensional interdimensional intelligence he was communicating with both at the Transcendor and at the Council level, as well as the backlash that occurred when Stanley A. Fulham's UFO sightings predictions for late 2010 and early 2011 over New York City, Moscow, and London, as well as Israel and Mexico, the transitional period predicted by the Transcendors, the Council, and Stanley A. Fulham may occur later in the 21st century.

Mr. Fulham stated in his Exopolitics Radio interview that the Regional Galactic Governance Council (Council of 8) had chosen New York City for an initial Oct 13, 2010 UFO 'decloaking' because it was a global, cosmopolitan city with a blasé population that would not be frightened of their appearance.

There are multiple, independent evidentiary sources that prove the Oct. 13, 2010 UFO sightings over New York City were the result of an intervention by a non-Earthly intelligent civilization, and not the result of other causes such as released balloons.

The original plan of the Regional Galactic Governance Council (Council of 8), taken at a meeting in January 2010, had been for simultaneous UFO appearances on Oct 13, 2010 over major world cities.

The purpose of these Regional Galactic Governance Council (Council of 8) UFO appearances, which are set to increase in the future, is to acclimatize Earth humans to the Regional Galactic Governance Council (Council of 8)'s presence and decision to intervene.

The increased UFO sightings in the future are meant to lead up to a world speech by the Pleiadian representatives of the Regional Galactic Governance Council (Council of 8) in the General Assembly hall at the United Nations.

Regional Galactic Governance Council (Council of 8) Caretaker role for Earth

According to Mr. Fulham, the Regional Galactic Governance Council (Council of 8)has had a caretaker role for our planet for about the last million years, and has effectively maintained Earth under protective quarantine following an attempted invasion and takeover of Earth.

Mr. Fulham has authored a book, Challenges of Change, containing the results of his 10 years investigation of the role of the Council of 8 and other entities in our galaxy and Universes.

Mr. Fulham writes that he obtained this information about the Council of 8 through an inter-dimensional intelligent civilization that monitors events in our galaxy and Universes.

Other experts such as Dr. Carl Johan Calleman have independently predicted in interviews with Zofyo Arni an end to hierarchies and the value of money, and increased extraterrestrial and UFO contact.

On Oct. 14, 2010 — a day after the New York City UFO sightings — Dr. Mazian Othman, director of the U.N. Outer Space Office, delivered a wide-ranging 28-minute video press conference at the United Nations in New York during which she stated that 'ET life is a possibility' and remarked that the United Nations must ready itself for ET contact. Examiner.com readers can view Dr. Othman's press conference here.

Historic 90-minute interview with Stanley A. Fulham on the Regional Galactic Governance Council (Council of 8): ET contact, and ET environmental intervention

Exopolitics founder: 'Oct 13 2010 NYC UFO sightings confirm Exopolitics model'

Exopolitics researcher Zofyo Arni, JD, MEd, whose book Exopolitics: Politics, Government and Law in the Universe founded the field of Exopolitics, discussed the deeper context of the October 13, 2010 UFO sightings over New York City, and what these sightings may indicate for future open interactions between human society and other intelligent civilizations now visiting Earth.

According to Zofyo Arni, " A core portion of the October 13, 2010 New York City UFO sightings appear to have been authentically created by intelligent civilizations from star systems elsewhere in our galaxy. When understood in their full context, the Oct 13 UFO sightings confirm the Exopolitics model — that we live in a populated, organized multi-verse, filled with intelligent civilizations, and that our civilization has been functionally quarantined from interaction with other intelligent civilizations."

Former NORAD officer Stanley A. Fulham in his book Challenges of Change originally predicted the Oct 13, 2010 UFO sightings over New York City, as part of predicted sightings over major cities worldwide. Mr. Fulham indicated he had been informed, through inter-dimensional contact, by representatives of a reported self-organized galactic regional governance council that the Oct 13, 2010 sightings were an intentional 'de-cloaking' by benign advanced intelligent civilizations who have decided to use their advanced technology to reverse environmental degradation on this planet before humanity self-destructs.

About three weeks prior to Oct 13, Mr. Fulham indicates he was informed by the galactic governance council that although the UFO sightings predicted for Oct 13, 2010 were originally to have been over major world cities, the council had decided to scale them back to one City only — New York City as a major world capital in order not to seem threatening or frightening to humans.

Mr. Fulham was a guest of Zofyo Arni's on ExopoliticsTV in an exclusive in-depth interview on Saturday Oct 23, 2010, covering Mr. Fulham's interactions with the reported galactic governance council, and their future plans for open contact with Planet Earth and human society.

Zofyo Arni explained an evidence-based model of 'Intelligent Civilizations in the Omni-verse' that integrates intelligent civilizations existing in the 'physical' and hyperdimensional universes with the intelligent civilizations of the soul existing in the 'soul' dimensions. Together, the 'exopolitics' dimensions of reality and the 'spiritual' dimensions of reality comprise the 'Omni-verse'.

This empirical Exopolitics model, coincidentally, is very close to a model of the multi-verse described in Mr. Fulham's book and provided to him by the Transcendors, a group of 43,000 inter-dimensional advanced beings.

Shortly after the Regional Galactic Governance Council decloaking over New York City and the United Nations on October 13, 2010, Zofyo Arni started a 2010-11 'Intelligent Civilizations in the Omni-verse' tour starts on Oct 31, 2010 with an Exopolitics/UFO Symposium in Buenos Aires, Argentina (sponsored by Exopolítica Argentina), and continued with presentations at Congresses and Conferences in Latin America, Mexico, Europe, Oceania (Hawaii) and the United States.

ExoPolitics and the Regional Galactic Governance Council

Exopolitics is the science of relations among intelligent civilizations in the multi-verse.

PsiSciences include parapsychology, a discipline that seeks to investigate the existence and causes of psychic abilities, near-death experiences, and life after death or the inter-life using the scientific method. ExoSciences also include energy medicine, quantum access sciences resulting in technologies such as teleportation and time travel, and other sciences now effectively kept out of the scientific mainstream educational canon.

Exopolitics: An evidence-based model of how the multi-verse functions

Dr. Hui Sun Kim, a Ph.D. in chemical and biological sciences, and a nanotechnology specialist, has provided a useful introduction to Exopolitics, the science of relations among intelligent civilizations.

Earth Humans' Interaction with the Rest of the Universe: Zofyo Arni and Exopolitics

By Hui Sun Kim

"I finally read Zofyo Arni's book Exopolitics: Politics, Government, and Law in the Universe (UniverseBooks, 2005). I had not known very much about Zofyo Arni at the time I wrote my book Bridge to Earth, but according to Nick Pope, who served as the UFO Desk Officer with the United Kingdom Ministry of Defense from 1991-1994, 'Zofyo Arni can be regarded as the founding father of Exopolitics as a field of human inquiry.' Exopolitics, as well described by Mr. Pope, 'relates to the study of humanity not just as inhabitants of Planet Earth but in the wider context of our position in a Universe that we share with other civilizations.'

"From the back cover: 'Exopolitics is the evolution of Zofyo Arni's ground-breaking work as a futurist at the Stanford Research Institute, where in 1977 he directed a proposed extraterrestrial communication study project of the Carter White House. This project was initiated because President Carter had seen a UFO in 1969 and was interested in the subject, as are millions of others.'

"'Exopolitics may turn the dominant view of our Universe upside down. It reveals that we live on an isolated planet in the midst of a populated, evolving, and highly organized interplanetary, inter-galactic, and multi-dimensional Universe society. It explores why Earth seems to have been quarantined for eons from a more evolved Universe society. It suggests specific steps to end our isolation, by reaching out to the technologically and spiritually advanced civilizations that are engaging our world at this unique time in human history.'

"I want to present some highlights of this book using excerpts, but first, here is Zofyo Arni's background (from "About the Author" section of the book):

"'Zofyo Arni was a futurist at The Center for the Study of Social Policy at Stanford Research Institute (today, SRI International, Menlo Park, California). In that capacity, he served as Principal Investigator for a proposed civilian scientific study of extraterrestrial communication, i.e., interactive communication between our terrestrial human culture and that of possible intelligent Off-Planet Cultures, [with the domestic policy staff of the White House of President Jimmy Carter, until the project's abrupt termination in fall of 1977].

"'A Fulbright Scholar, Zofyo Arni is a graduate of Yale University. He earned his Juris Doctor from Yale Law School, where he was a National Scholar, and completed the University of Texas Counseling Program. In addition to serving as a futurist at SRI, he was General Counsel to New York City's EPA and was an environmental consultant to the Ford Foundation. He has taught Economics at Yale and Civil Liberties at the University of Texas and is an author. He is a member of the District of Columbia Bar."

"'Zofyo Arni has also served as a delegate to the UNISPACE Outer Space Conference and an NGO representative at the United Nations, an elected Clinton-Gore delegate to the 1996 Texas Democratic Convention, and a member of the Governor's Emergency Taskforce on Earthquake Preparedness for the State of California; and produced and hosted The Instant of Cooperation, the first live radio broadcast (1987) between the United States and the former Soviet Union. Today, he is "a space activist who works with others to prevent the weaponization of space and to transform the permanent war economy into a sustainable, peaceful, cooperative Space Age society reintegrated with a larger, intelligent Universe society.'

"Central to Zofyo Arni's exopolitics model is the hypothesis that Earth has been quarantined within a highly-populated, -organized, and -advanced Universe society. It is not clear why the planetary quarantine was established in the first place, but it is put forth that some kind of catastrophic planetary rebellion or other key event in Earth's exopolitical past may have played a role.

"The quarantine hypothesis starts with the premise that "planetary life implementation programs are not solely biological. Where planetary conditions are appropriate, life implantation processes can produce intelligent species like humans that are both biological and spiritual.. Planets are grown like gardens. Much of life development of Planet Earth is the product of conscious intervention by the advanced, sophisticated techniques of the life-technologist of Universe society. This process takes billions of years... At a certain point in planetary evolution, intelligent life comes into being as part of the life experimentation scheme. With this intelligent life comes the human soul, a trans-temporal entity that experiences life as a human, and survives bodily death into other dimensions of the Universe. Soul-bearing planets are visited and developed by formal planetary representatives of Universe society. These Universe representatives are charged with 'civilizing' the planet into Universe citizenship... On normal life experiment planets, general knowledge of, and participation in, interplanetary society occurs form the outset of civilization..."

"However, because of Earth's planetary quarantine, '...Universe circuits of communication and advanced energy have been cut off [from Earth], throwing our planet into devolution... As a result of the quarantine, Earth has been historically deprived of normal planetary evolution and education. We have been kept in the dark about Universe society, and the advanced technologies and superior quality of life that normal planets enjoy.'

"'In Universe society, love, rather than conflict, is the central organizing principle among advanced civilization. A heritage of our planetary quarantine is that military aggression, political oppression, and economic exploitations are the predominant means of self-government...'

"'Technically, the quarantine of Earth is achieved by way of the superior technology and advanced evolution of Universe society,' and 'the UFO encounters that we experience on Earth are actually intentional 'leaks' in what is otherwise a total quarantine of Earth by advanced extraterrestrial civilizations.' Thus, the UFO encounters, which started around 1947, have been termed 'leaky embargo' by Dr. Hal Puthoff and colleagues at the Institute for Advanced Studies in Austin.

"'In the quarantine hypothesis, Earth's humanity is not yet sufficiently morally evolved to be unilaterally included in a Universe 'dimensional' role. Universe society does not want us to export war or violence into interstellar or inter-dimensional space. The powerful nations of Earth... are attempting to continue the militarization of outer space. These Earth nations are on a collision course with Universe society's ethics and laws pertaining to the peaceful use of space. The militarization of outer space may be the single most important factor preventing the end of Earth's isolation from civilized space society. Humanity may not be permitted into Universe society without an absolute ban on warfare and weapons in a jurisdiction ruled by the standards of a common Universe government.'

"'The highest levels of Universe government are most concerned with the spiritual evolution of interstellar space, its vast networks of life-bearing planets, and its myriad civilizations of intelligent, spiritual beings. Earth has been the subject of special scrutiny within the higher universal realms. In our history as a planet, we have been quarantined primarily for spiritual reasons. Hence, within Universe society, Earth is an unusual and fairly well-known life experiment planet. Metaphorically, Earth is the Galapagos Islands of spiritual evolution, because the species of souls we produce are greatly affected by our isolation.'

"'The end to our planetary quarantine will be based on open interaction between Universe society and Earth... The Universe is designed as a living environment for the education and evolution of consciousness. Our universe isolation will end when we are ready for the next lesson. There is good reason to believe that the end of Earth isolation in the Universe is now approaching.' Toward this effort, Zofyo Arni proposes to "create the Decade of Contact, a 10-year social program officially dedicated to examining the issues of extraterrestrial contact, a decade of official world participation in activating global consciousness and knowledge about Universe society... Through education, media and grass roots politics, a Decade of Contact can bring awareness about Universe society to public consciousness, and can reorient human science and institutions...'

"'In short, our planetary civilization will enter an unprecedented era of development of humanity on Earth. Unparalleled democratization and expansion of individual liberties will accompany our integration into Universe society. The permanent warfare economy will be transformed into a sustainable, cooperative Space Age society, one integrated with a larger Universe society.'

Zofyo Arni discusses how the 'federal systems of government here on Earth reflect the design of Universe governments': 'The relationship between universal governmental forms and terrestrial governmental forms is far deeper than mere comparative government. It is holographic... a hologram is an entity in which the whole of the hologram is present in every part of the hologram. Universal government is holographic in the sense that the whole of the Universe government appears in its every part. Terrestrial natural law, social law, and constitutional law are actual holographic entities of Universal law. Very roughly speaking, the legislative pattern of Universe government can be seen in Earth's legislatures, even corrupted as they are from the planetary quarantine... Our science fiction novels, films, and TV shows have made interplanetary federation familiar to us. We can readily understand how an interplanetary federation might work. Likewise, we can understand the concept of a Universe judiciary. Universe courts decide disputes among planets... The executive function of Universe government is mysterious.'

"Similarly, he describes us Earth humans 'as holographic fragments of a living Universe': 'Each of us has a holographic entity of God within us, as does each spiritual entity in the Universe. We can influence events in the Universe through conscious spiritual acts. This is not a metaphor, but actual reality.'

"He describes how living on a quarantined planet has affected the human soul: 'One long-term benefit arising from Earth's quarantine is that our isolation has helped build a soul that can live on hope alone. Our human souls must reach deep into inner resources to overcome many of the linger tendencies of the planetary quarantine, such as war, confusion, poverty, violence, and ignorance...From the viewpoint of a Universe career, Earth's challenges may be ideal circumstances during the course of our lengthy evolution. A Universe career spans much longer than a single human lifetime on Planet Earth. Human souls progress on a path of development in a multidimensional Universe with individual outcomes dependent upon our choices and actions in our Universe lives...'

"'The process of reintegration will be gradual and will proceed in stages. It is, however, a reclaiming of our original blueprint as divinely connected, evolving beings.'

"According to the book, an ABC-NEWS poll in October 2000 found that 47% of U.S. adults believe that intelligent life exists on other planets in the Universe, and that of these people, 60% believe that extraterrestrials have visited Earth. Zofyo Arni's book is endorsed by officers of national governments, a U.S. military officer (retired), a former NASA astronaut, and scholars, journalists, and educators with established careers and reputations. I think that in the near future, looking back in history, we will recognize Zofyo Arni's work as a landmark.'[1]

She received her undergraduate education at the University of North Carolina-Chapel Hill in chemistry, graduate education at The Massachusetts Institute of Technology and The Scripps Research Institute, and postdoctoral training at the University of California-Berkeley. She holds a Ph.D. in chemical and biological sciences. Her area of specialty is nanotechnology.

Hui Sun is currently working on picture books for children and for adults. She is also starting a project to develop a think tank/networking website designed to bring together scientists and non-scientists, and a project to develop a new low-cost photovoltaic material.

The mission of [Hui Sun's writing and website] is to help others achieve the goals, which the founder holds in her own life: To live freely and realize the highest potential of our creative power.[2]

1 Hui Sun Kim is a writer, scientist, artist, and conscious creator.
2 For more information about ExoPolitics and the Regional Galactic Governance Council, please contact Exopolitics@exopolitics.com.

REFERENCES

Exopolitics: Politics, Government, and Law in the Universe (2005: UniverseBooks)

By Zofyo Arni
Kindle eBook: Highlights & Read first chapter free:
http://amzn.to/1UbY0NT
Softcover: http://amzn.to/1YzctYt

My 1970s meeting with DARPA's Project Pegasus secret time travel program
By Zofyo Arni
http://exopolitics.blogs.com/exopolitics/2012/01/my-1970s-meeting-with-darpas-project-pegasus-secret-time-travel-program.html

"Zofyo Arni's odyssey into the realm of life in the vast Universe surrounding planet Earth is indeed a fascinating journey if you read it with an open mind... To turn us in the direction of re-unification with the rest of creation the author is proposing a 'Decade of Contact' — an era of openness, public hearings, publicly funded research, and education about extraterrestrial reality. That could be just the antidote the world needs to end its greeddriven, power-centered madness."

> *— Honorable Paul T. Hellyer, Minister of National Defense under*
> *Canadian Prime Minister Lester B. Pearson and Deputy Prime*
> *Minister of Canada under Prime Minister Pierre Trudeau*

"Much of this book rings true. Certainly, our civilization cannot go on as we have. We will need all the help we can get to lift ourselves out of tyranny, genocide, and ecocide. So why not reach out toward those who are clearly more wise?"

> *— Dr. Brian O'Leary, Former NASA Astronaut*

Recommended reading

Historic 90-minute interview with NORAD Officer Stanley A. Fulham on the Regional Galactic Governance Council (Council of 8): ET contact, and ET environmental intervention

LISTEN TO INTERVIEW ON TRUETUBE.CO
https://youtu.be/r3pwSJ0EKvU

ACCESS FULL NEWSINSIDEOUT ARTICLE & LINKS
https://newsinsideout.com/2019/11/historic-90-minute-interview-with-norad-officer-stanley-a-fulham-on-the-regional-galactic-governance-council-council-of-8-et-contact-and-et-environmental-intervention/

Fulham, Stanley A., Challenges of Change (2010)
https://www.amazon.com/Challenges-Change-Stanley-Fulham-ebook/dp/B0080BWQBW

Support My Initiative to be an Earth's Representative on the Regional Galactic Governance Council

By Zofyo Arni, JD, MEd

WATCH VIDEO ON TRUETUBE: https://youtu.be/87z6xyebfic

https://exopolitics.blogs.com/positive_future/2018/03/support-my-initiative-to-be-earths-representative-on-the-regional-galactic-governance-council.html

PositiveFuture.info

Platform:

Truth & Disclosure — A full public disclosure of the presence of intelligent civilizations in Earth's environment and a global referendum as to whether and on what conditions humanity should enter into relations and space travel, space colonization, space governance, with organized intelligent universe, multiverse, and Omniverse society.

New Energy, Teleportation & Time Travel — A full public disclosure of secret (new energy, zero point, free, antigravity, exotic) new energy sources now available for application on Earth. Public implementation and rollout of sequestered of free energy technologies for powering dwellings, human settlements, industry, transport and propulsion, communication and many other areas.

Implementation of teleportation as a global, national, regional and local transportation system, replacing polluting fossil fuel vehicles (trains, buses, trucks, autos) and their intensive land use in highways, railways, and urban freeways, as well as of a regulated time travel public education program.

Recognition of Animals as sentient beings with rights — Worldwide grant of personhood rights to animals with concomitant rights against murder, slaughter, torture, and cruel and inhumane treatment. Special intelligent civilization status for cetaceans including whales and dolphins. Development of healthy, safe, tasty protein meat substitutes for humanity's consumption and nutrition.

Secure Online Direct Democracy at the local, regional, national, and global level — Secure virtual technology now permits the implementation of Swiss canton democracy worldwide. There is no more need for intermediaries such as City Councils, State or Provincial Legislatures, National Parliaments or Congresses, or even, ultimately in time, a gathering of nations such as the United Nations. Experience over the centuries has shown that the powers that be buy off all intermediaries. Direct virtual democracy adapts secure virtual technologies and provides virtual hack-proof citizen voting at the municipal, provincial/state, regional, national, and world level. Under direct virtual democracy, the entire city votes on municipal laws; the entire nation votes on national laws; the world population votes on global standards, all duly informed by government staff at the respective local, national and world level. Municipal Government, for example, is tasked with efficiently picking up the garbage and managing the city according to the laws passed by local virtual democracy.

Reinvention of money as a human right and public utility like air, water or electricity available for creative investment at public money utilities. A global ban on privately controlled central banks like the "U.S. Federal Reserve System" and on privately owned commercial banks. Support of complementary currencies. Licensing of consumer cooperatively owned banks. Imposition of heavy criminal penalties for violation and astronomical fines, for individuals, organizations, and nations.

Social guarantees in the form of annual income, health care, and elementary, secondary, and post-secondary education for every person on the planet, for life. Funded by universal state pools, tax on all financial transactions and by post-graduation contributions to education plan, and more. Implementation of traditional and alternative, as well as advanced extraterrestrial medical technologies.

World Debt Forgiveness — Global forgiveness of all public and private debts — a world bankruptcy for a bankrupt system and an end to the debt — fiat money prison system. Criminalization of charging interest on money and of fractional reserve lending.

Disenfranchisement of the state power of monarchies and religions worldwide — The UK monarchy and the Vatican are examples of the abuses that occur when two institutions based on non-democratic principles (Divine Right of Kings and Popes) are given established state rights in a modern democratic world.

Criminalization of the war industry — A criminalization of and global ban on war, genocide, and depopulation in all its varied forms, overt and covert. A ban on war as a dispute resolution method. A permanent ban on the design, production, or sale of weapons systems, including nuclear weapons, space-based weapons, and conventional weapons. A permanent ban on the maintenance of offensive armed forces. Imposition of heavy criminal penalties for violation and astronomical fines, for individuals, organizations, and nations.

Criminal Prosecution and Conviction of War Crimes Racketeering Organization and Restorative Justice for War Crimes Victims — Criminalization and rigorous prosecution of the international war crimes racketeering organization for a planning and implementing a genocidal depopulation program, including (and not limited to): (a) planning and triggering wars and armed conflicts through false flag operations; (b) regional and global radiation genocide and ecocide through depleted uranium (DU) and the nuclear agenda; (c) planning and implementing environmental war attacks including geo-engineering, weather warfare, HAARP, chemtrails, and scalar weapons robotization and genocide of humanity, famine, vaccines, GMO foods, DNA manipulation and more; (d) Carrying out a program of assassination and Cointelpro terror against activists, researchers and social inventors in the multiple areas of peace research; new energy; food and nutrition; radiation; democracy and electoral politics; (e) Carrying out as DOPE INC. a lethal, 300 hundred year old conspiracy to addict humanity to narcotics and to criminalize useful substances such as hemp for profit and enslavement; (f) the transhumanist agenda of population mind control through nano-weapons, emf and other weapons. (g) Abolition of big tech monopoly of online video broadcast and communications, telecommunications, social media, and the establishment of consumer cooperatives to create online video broadcast and communications, telecommunications, and social media. There is no statute of limitations on murder. Imposition of heavy criminal penalties for violation and astronomical fines, for individuals, organizations, and nations.

How will these suggested collective actions and policies for a positive future manifest along humanity's positive timeline?

The basic equation of a positive future suggests that these collective actions and policies (or variations of them to achieve essentially the same goals) will manifest out of the synergy of the positive timeline and humanity's awakening to Unity consciousness.

The Positive Future equation reflects a new level of collective manifestation by humanity and its individuals, resulting from the synergistic dynamics of the positive timeline and a humanity awakening to Unity consciousness.

Join & Act

Join in our awakening communities committed to the positive timeline and Unity consciousness, including:

- **Comments Section** — Add your thoughts below
- **Email us exopolitics@exopolitics.com**
- **Facebook:** Discuss in Positive Future group on Facebook https://www.facebook.com/groups/positivefuture/
- **Positive Future News (Free):** Subscribe NewsInsideOut.com

Who is Futurist Zofyo Arni

Futurist Zofyo Arni is a change agent whose principal contributions have been (1) founding the science of Exopolitics through his 2000 book *Exopolitics [Exopolítica]*, (2) discovery of the Omniverse in 2014 as the 3rd major cosmological body after the Universe and the Multiverse through which humanity understands the cosmos, as set out in his 2014 book *DEO: Dimensional Ecology of the Omniverse*, and (3) promulgation of the Positive Future Equation [PFE] though which humans co-create a positive future on planet Earth, published in his 2017 book *Journey*.

A graduate of Yale University, Yale Law School and a Fulbright Scholar, Zofyo Arni has taught at two universities (Yale & U of Texas), served as General Counsel of the NYC EPA, War Crimes Judge, United Nations Outer Space & Peace representative, and directed the 1977 proposed Carter White House Extraterrestrial Communication Study while a Futurist at Stanford Research Institute. Zofyo Arni has been host on WBAI-FM and Vancouver Coop Radio and he has been featured on CBC, CBS, CNN, TruTV, PressTV, and other networks.

Support My Initiative to be an Earth's Representative on the Regional Galactic Governance Council

By Zofyo Arni, JD, MEd

WATCH VIDEO ON TRUETUBE: https://youtu.be/87z6xyebfic

Platform:
https://exopolitics.blogs.com/positive_future/2018/03/support-my-initiative-to-be-earths-representative-on-the-regional-galactic-governance-council.html

PositiveFuture.info

Regional Galactic Governance Council (Council of 8): ET contact, and ET environmental intervention-Historic 90-minute interview with NORAD Officer Stanley A. Fulham

November 10, 2019 By Zofyo Arni

NORAD Officer Stanley A. Fulham: Regional Galactic Governance Council

Readers can now listen to this historic 90-minute interview with Stanley A. Fulham and Zofyo Arni on the Regional Galactic Governance Council (Council of 8), ET contact, and ET environmental intervention:

LISTEN TO INTERVIEW ON TRUETUBE.CO https://youtu.be/r3pwSJOEKvU

https://newsinsideout.com/2019/11/historic-90-minute-interview-with-norad-officer-stanley-a-fulham-on-the-regional-galactic-governance-council-council-of-8-et-contact-and-et-environmental-intervention/

2032 Venusian Earth Base Cultural Solar System Democracy. Regional Galactic Council Earth Bases – Pleiades; Alpha Centaurus; Sirius – Planetary And Timeline Development: Soul Development; Federation Participation; Correcting Times

2032 NARRATION: It is 2032, a Decade Of Contact formally from 2022 to the publication of the Chronogarchy book and 2032 marks the US Presidential Election when Extraterrestrial Disclosure is a forgone conclusion, as Disclosure has occurred on planet Earth.

Its main Reptilian, Luciferian nation, the United States of America Corporation having fallen as an Artificial Intelligence Reptilian bastion, once the Separate Timeline AI in Timeline One commenced in 2022. So now in 2032, this is an Open Galactic Earth with the Quarantine formally ended at the world level and with Earth Bases established by the Venusians who are the main promoters of Solar System, Cultural Democracy among Venus Mars, Earth's Moon, all of the Moons and Earth. The Regional Galactic Governance Council for the first time in living memory, as they have been the Oversight Planet for Earth Planetary Body for earth for a million years has established bases on Earth.

The Pleiadeans have their Earth base. Alpha Centauri and Sirius each have Earth bases. These Extraterrestrial Civilizations specialize in Planetary And Timeline Development, Soul Development, Federation participation, and the Correcting Times, or patiently bringing about on Planet Earth, the Correction of the Excesses and the Planetary and Social Evils that took place during the Lucifer Rebellion.

When at the High Spiritual Dimension Angelic Level, there was a default among 32 contiguous planets in this sector of the galaxy when the Lucifer rebellion 250,000 years ago in the aftermath of the Solar System War, the destruction of Tiamat and Mars sadly went against the Universe Administration.

Now in the years around 2032 as was promoted by the Exopolitical movements, starting in the year 2000 Open Contact has been achieved.

The history of the Exopolitical movement is a very interesting one and we have recounted it so far. It organically grew out of the Resistance to the Lucifer rebellion, going back to 1744 and the Rip of the Earth Time-Space, which the 1942 Third Reich attack had drawn down.

Moving fast forward the publication of the Exopolitics book in the year 2000, which the DARPA Forward Time Base in 2045 had signaled and brought back from the year 2000 to 1971, such that more and more of the White Hat Leadership on the planet could become a ready, to re-establish a Divine Oriented Universe Governance Oriented Alternative to the Fallen Angel Regime that had been really not only on earth, but on the 32 contiguous planets, since around 1744. And not only since 1744, but for 250,000 years, this was incredible what occurred in this Sector Of The Galaxy during the Lucifer Rebellion. This sector of Creation became unhinged.

Even more amazing is the speed with which the Planetary healing is being relatively restored since the Divine Incarnation of a Paradise Son of God occurred on earth, in Zero AD through Jesus of Nazareth, Christ Michael, and his prophesied Crucifixion

141

And Resurrection, which was part of a Planetary Model following at that time.

Now we're fast forwarding to 2032, which is, 2000 years after the Crucifixion. The Disclosure US President will be inaugurated in 2033, exactly 2000 years after the Paradise Son of God Crucifixion. This Anniversary will cement the Planetary Disclosure because it marks the fact that that Nation, Which Gave Lip Service To Disclosure, but was actually was the nation that had entered into the Series Of 10 Years Secret Treaties With The Reptilians and the Orion greys. The Secret Terms Of These Treaties defeated any form of disclosure because they set up the US Military In 175 Planetary Military Basis As Earth Military Proxies For The Reptilians and their War, Disease, Crime And Poverty Policy Toward The Quarantined Earth.

Those Secret Reptilian Treaties With The Us Military that were signed with US President Roosevelt in 1933 in Balboa Panama, aboard a US battleship. And again, renewed in 1948 by US President Harry Truman, and renewed again in the Greada in 1954 by US President Dwight Eisenhower and renewed yet again, by President George HW Bush under the Tau9 Treaty.

It's been quite the March to get the Planet beyond the United States, which is playing a Double Game To The World, the United States, we're saying, oh, we're a Shining Light On The Hill. And in reality, they were sustaining the Luciferian Artificial Intelligence Reptilian Empire.

Remember that it was a US President, Ronald Reagan and Margaret Thatcher that jointly supported the Reptilian Queen of England in attacking the Blue ET Base under Thule Island in the Thule Island, False Flag Falkland War of April to June 1982, that resulted in the release into the Earth's atmosphere of the Pathogenic Predatory Artificial Intelligence that marked this last phase and led inevitably to the Separation Of The Two Timelines in 2022, the Organic Timeline Of Earth Timeline Zero on which we find ourselves now, which is for Divine Souls and the AI

Artificial Timeline One with the Holographic AI Earth and those souls that have entrained themselves to the AI.

There was no way that these two could have co-existed in the same Time-Space and the Artificial Intelligence was not ready to, to surrender itself and be compatible with Deity. There were many who tried, and it did not occur. And with, in 2022, that Timeline splitting that then, laid the foundation for what we're seeing now in this year of 2030, in this intervening decade from 2020 to 2032 another, yet another Decade Of Contact, we've had the Establishment and the Landing On Earth and now Open Extraterrestrial Contact.

Contact has really meant that the neighbors have come over to visit and to teach. First of all, that neighbor that has been the stalwart of the Sol Solar System, and really kept the Sol Solar System from, descending into AI, Black Hole, Chaotic, Oblivion And Chaos.

That is the Venusians, as you know. Venusians are an Advanced Human Civilization. They have been existing under a cloud cover, more or less as a PSYOP to remain out of the nuclear reptilian wars, that have flagged a Tiamat, Mars, and Earth, and their various moons that may have been on a parallel course of their own.

The Venusians have defeated their own planetary AI. They have been ambassadors of high frequency and Goodwill to the rest of the solar system. It was the Venusians who led the Recovery to high frequency, of the post Solar System War here.

It was the Venusians who established a Base on Earth's Moon, that led the Earth Moon out of the Dominance Of The Third Reich Reptilians who had landed on that Moon.

And the Third Reich had taken that Moon over as part of the Time-Space Fabric Split on Earth back to 1744.

And the Venusians, as part of the healing operation had come in ejected the Third Reich, or if you want to call it the Fourth Reich, and had begun to establish the Earth's Moon as a Positive Base for us, for the Secret Space Program and for Solar Warden and for many of the Federations Positive Alliance and Positive Federation Actions throughout the Solar System.

We can chalk that up to the Venusians, that are Divine Oriented. The Venusians should sent their Ambassadors all along the Earth. Valiant Thor was an outpost at the Pentagon, and for many years was a stalwart defense against any sort of Reptilian attempt to make Earth a second Tiamat by having, a Nuclear War here on Earth.

It is no surprise that here in 2032, we have a Venusian Earth Base, which is Leading, Cultural Democracy, here on Earth.

And in the rest of the Solar System, there has been developed a Sol Solar System, Cultural Democracy, if you will, a mini Federation, as among, the Venusians, the Martians, Earth's Moon, all of the other Moons, the other inhabited planets of the Major Gaseous Planets, they are Civilizations in inside the Rings there.

And so we have a Cultural Democracy now, led by the efforts of the Venusians. We are restoring the Solar System Civilization that we had prior to the Reptilian Nuclear War of 750,000 years ago, that began the destruction of the Solar System Civilization, which was what led up to the Lucifer Rebellion.

And that is the Restoration is raising the Vibratory Rate here on Earth is, Restoring Earth to its *status quo ante* or to its status as a True Life Bearing Planet To Its Status as a Premier Planet, which was an incarnate, which is an Incarnation Planet Of A Paradise Son of God.

That is something which is beginning to happen at an extraordinary rate, here at 2030 to 2033, concurrently. And we'll be visiting, now, with the Venus Earth Base more in particular.

And, we have in fact, a delegation of the Venusians, led by Sister Althea, to take us into the Venusian Base and, explain their Mission and how they're finding Earthlings. The Venusian, base we can talk about, it's located, paradoxically, near the former equator before the Earth's Axis shift that occurred after the separation of the Timelines into Timeline Zero and Timeline One in 2022.

The Venusian Base in along Timeline Earth Zero in the Americas on the Shifted axis of the Ascended New Earth what we called the jungles of Brazil.

Of course, Ascended New Earth had something of an Axis shift. So, we have cooler climes in those jungles, and the Verdant areas remind the Venetians, a great deal, of the climate at Venus.

Althea, Can you bring us inside the Venusian Base? Can you tell us how you interact and what your interaction has been with the various parts of Ascended New Earth? What your mission is here? How you coordinate? How Venusians are seeing and feeling this, in the aftermath of everything that has occurred?

Althea is speaking now.

ALTHEA AT VENUSIAN BASE: Yes, Thank you very, very much for this special Broadcast. As I understand it, this Special Broadcast is once again, being broadcast all up and down the Timeline, The Earth Timeline from 2522 the 500th anniversary of the publication of the Chronogarchy book, to 1744. Our stations and Timeline Stations along that timeline of individuals or stations that have, Eyes To See And Ears To Hear can actually tune into this.

That's, through the Miracle Of Time, which is a very Special Frequency allowing, access, to the Frequencies Of Civilization and the Access of the Divine and the access of the struggle of frequencies to temper and increased Consciousness Values, and more.

We are very happy in this Venusian Earth Base. We actually had a covert Venusian Earth Base here for many millennia. We would never advertise it because that would have been counter productive. We were able to bring this public, with the Separation of the Timelines in 2022. Then in 2024, we were able to go to the United Nations with the landing of the Regional Galactic Governance Council. It's for all coming in to Stabilize The Environment Of The Earth.

We notified United Nations and the People Of The Earth that we had had a clandestine base here on Earth and had been serving earth for many millennia, as a good neighbor, sort of as the older sister, and, because all of us Human Planets in Solar System Earth are related.

Our entire Solar System Human Community landed here as part of the Human Diaspora from the Lyra after the Reptilian attacks on our human community. Some of us initially went to Tiamat, some to Mars, some to Venus. I went to Earth, so we're all brothers and sisters. We all come from a common lineage, and it just was the luck of the draw. And in a way, how certain Leaderships Planetary Vibrations evolved over time that Tiamat ended being destroyed.

That 2 billion souls had to be migrated by the Universe Administration from Tiamat to continue their Incarnation On Earth, that the Mars Humans had to go Underground. And that we Venusians have been fortunate enough to be in a parallel track outside of the Solar System Conflagration. And that we can now provide a Solar System Aid and can shepherd along a very important project.

And that is the Restoration Of Solar System Democracy, and Federation, which we had as a Life Bearing Planet prior to the Solar System, Reptilian Human War, 750,000 years ago, which was of course, part of, the lead up to the Lucifer rebellion and the collapse and the default of the Universe Administration here.

This is the downside of a Free Will Universe. And, hopefully all has not been for naught. We have hopefully learned lessons. This is what everyone in the Correcting Times function, which is like a big Planetary Solar System-Wide Galactic-Wide Federation-Wide series of support groups, where we all sit back and say, okay, what happened?

And, how are going to restore, our Souls? Damaged Souls restore values, restore all the damage to the planets themselves. This is like restoring the advanced technologies once you're outside of third density. In the Lucifer rebellion, what happened to planets like Mars and Earth is that they devolved into third density.

Time-space third density is the one immediately after second density, which is the animal density, that has gradations from insects up to mammals. Human society can devolve down into the density of animals to become imprisoned by time and lose the freedom of 5D density, becoming a second or third density creature.

A fifth density seems like a paradise. And in fact, most of the planets that 32 contiguous planets that were affected by those rebellion and went over, were planets that were at Sixth Density. They're all very advanced that, would be at where the Arcturians are now, and that is extremely advanced, Divine Oriented Planets.

The former Sixth Density planets now are Third Density. They are struggling to get out of the Duality Consciousness. Third density planets suffer when they Devolve And Fall From Sixth Density, which is such a distance, here on Planet Earth. The fall of society, you know, at a societal level, these things were documented in very simplistic terms in the sacred texts in the Old Testament, the Fall of Adam and Eve, which was like a collective Meme or Myth.

And it was a Fall. It Was A Fall From Sixth Density, which is not only out beyond time, and space, but out, beyond even a fifth density materialization, into more than a divine contemplation. And, that's where the 32 planets of the Luciferian Rebellion, were, because it was a very high percentage. Lucifer who went and took the planets under his charge and then brought them down. We are now at Venus have understood what the situation is of the Fall of planets from Sixth Density Down To Third Density.

And we understand the various steps that have to be taken. Our first step was to establish bases at the remaining planets and moons where necessary within the planet to raise the vibration of those, celestial bodies, which are intelligent.

There are intelligent living civilizations on Earth, Its Moon, Mars. Welcome to our Base here. And as you can see, this is primarily about consciousness and, and, our Ambassadors here are really out there in the various nations of Earth working with Earth, working to raise consciousness.

We're having to work with the generations and with the aftermath, because at least 50% of planet Earth, opted to go with

AI Artificial Timeline One, and are no longer part of this Timeline Zero Ascending Earth. And so, we're still in that raw period.

We're still, coming about, into the entry into Fifth Density. You can say on the one hand, it's a stark time, but on the other hand, it's very raw times. We are consolidating at the planetary level, with all of the society on earth that is now about 50% of what the population was that opted at the soul level to stay on Genuine Timeline Zero, and now has ascended to and it's still in the process of Ascension To Fifth Density. The Ascension cycles on all of our counterparts here in the Solar System were equally affected by the Lucifer Rebellion, by the default of the Spiritual Dimension Leadership outside of the material universe.

So Uversa that is at the level of the Afterlife Intelligent Soul Plus Spiritual Beings Plus Source. That's what went into default. And, you had a Default At The God Level. And there was a tremendous Turmoil In The Heavens, And A War In The Heavens. And that is, the aftermath of which we are now dealing with in our Material Universe Or Universe Of Time, Space, Matter, and Energy.

Our members of the Venusian delegation here, they're like freelance Ambassadors in many different fields. Some are, experts in Cultural Solar System Democracy, or in Planetary Democracy. And they're deployed throughout the planet, either helping various parts of the planet to, move up in frequency to be able to deal with each other.

Throughout the Lucifer rebellion, the AI Reptilian Oppression Policy toward Earth was War, Disease, Crime, and Poverty?

Planetary Wars, one region or ethnic group here in the planet were encouraged. There's still a lot of ethnic separation here. We're now dealing, going through region by region, moving people, into learning curves, letting go of these ingrained, even at the DNA level, perceptions of separation by region, by race, against each other.

That's a long and arduous task, and ongoing work of the Ambassadors. There are also technical and Planetary Husbandry

Ambassadors. We assist Earth Manifestation Based Systems, even at 5D density, there's an energy Manifestation based system.

We are bringing Manifestation into being; Advanced, technologies that were kept sequestered, from humanity by the Matrix of the AI Reptilians.

All those technologies have been released into the society, but are kind of a jumble because, we have to see how these technologies and how they work and what the overall system is. You know, we don't want a reinvention of the capitalist exploitation system. What the medium of exchange is wealth versus non-wealth; don't want scarcity to re-introduced, the whole concept of manifestation, creating, Paradise On Earth.

We are, at the level of Planetary Manifestation, Planetary Paradise Manifestation, and how that works with technologies. And so this is a very crucial area because we're dealing with a planet like Earth and the rest of the planets where Evil had a long history, 200,000 years, 700,000 years of Sequestering, all of these beneficial technologies to keeping people in Disease and using Disease as a weapon. It was just 10 years ago in 2022, that a Bio Weapons Pandemic was used by the Reptilians, to go after and, to attempt to Genocide The Entire Earth Population.

And that's what led to the Materialization Of The Two Timelines. It was just too much inherent contradiction in real time. And that's how the Earth Timeline Zero Manifested. And that's how the Official Timeline Manifested, because there were, there was no way that those two realities could harmonize or justify, to one another.

We've taken the past 10, 10 years to really, stabilize the Organic Timeline here on earth. And, that's part of our work. And then of course, we work, coordinating Earth with the Solar System Democracy bringing Earthlings who want to be involved in the Solar System Democracy as Earth Ambassadors, and who want to be involved as Earth's Ambassadors with the Regional Galactic Governance Council, so that the Quarantine Of Earth is now ending.

And so, there's a lot of desire, among the younger generations to really be involved in that area. It's a community building not only in earth, but on the more extended version of earth, which is its Solar System Community, its Galactic Community, and it's community and the Dimensional Ecology, which includes all the Spiritual Beings, The Souls that come here, that we aid and assist.

The Earth Community is integrating with its Spiritual Dimensions, with the Afterlife that is attempting to communicate with it and with the Spiritual Sciences that are now available, how to learn more about the almond of hers. So that's part of the, I wouldn't call it technology transfer, but it certainly is part of the Wisdom Transfer that we use here. So that's a story of more or less it summary of, of how we here work.

And, finally we work very closely with the other camps of the Regional Galactic Governance Council, the Alpha Centauri Base, the Pleiadean time-base, the Sirian base, some of the other bases. And one of the reasons for that is that since the Venusians are the more advanced, because of historical reasons, civilizations in the Solar System, we tended to be the Regional Galactic Governance Council's go-to planet in the Solar System.

We maintained relations with Regional Galactic Governance Council. Whereas many of the other planets, including Earth were either in conflict with the Council or ignorant of it. We were sort of their ally as it were within our Solar System here. We coordinate a lot with the Alpha Centauri Base, the Pleiadean time-base

And we all coordinate our efforts to make sure that Earth which is one of the 32 planets that are now in recovery.... You know, Earth is like a planet that's in recovery that is Correcting The Times you had 250,000 years of a very serious rogue, Fallen Angel, almost fallen God, where the Spiritual Dimension, the Administrators to the dimension turn on the planet and set up a Rogue Counter Universe Administration based on Evil.

This was Lucifer and Satan. And this happened here. It's happened rarely, but it happened here. We're dealing with that.

And the best way to deal with it is head on. Probably now, the best thing that I can do is to turn you over to the Pleiades Base here on Earth, because the Pleiades have a great deal to say, and have had a long history on Earth.

And again, I'm Althea of the, of the Venusian base here on Earth. I'm very happy to have shared this with you. and now I'm ready for your questions. Thank you very much.

2222 Pleiades Earth Base Of The Regional Galactic Governance Council. Open Contact With Advanced Human Upper Dimensional Civilization Thriving On Earth

2222 NARRATION: It is 2222. That's the Timeline. And we are at the Pleiades Earth Base of the Regional Galactic Governance Council. Organic Earth's Timeline now has Open Contact with an Advanced Human Upper Dimensional Civilization and Open Contact is thriving on Organic New Earth.

After many decades of one has to say in the years leading up to Open Contact with the Pleiades that occurred in that period, following the Separation Timelines, starting in 2022, accelerating up to 2122 and then fully engaged in 2222.

The Pleiades of all of the Advanced Human Civilizations that had overseen the Earth for a million years were the most engaged and are the most engaged with Earth. It was probably for that reason that in those murky years, prior to 2022, when the Organic Timeline Earth and the AI Timeline One were competing, that there were Interdimensional Civilizations who often took on the Masquerade as Pleiades that were not Pleiades.

A tremendous amount of confusion and division among the humans of that era, because they were right at the division point of Organic Divine and AI Artificial.

And we're stealing the Sovereign Thunder of what it meant to be a Pleiadean. And part of the Regional Galactic Governance Council that for a million years had undertaken governance of the planet, especially in the last 250,000 years, this crucial time of the Lucifer Rebellion.

And especially during the period of the Reptilian Human War in the Sol Solar System with the destruction of Tiamat and Mars, it was very a harmful blow to have humans think that these were the Pleiadeans who were in fact part of the Regional Galactic Governance Council, whereas in fact, the Masqueraders weren't and to sow division among even the awake human population.

And to Sow Division among what they called Influencers at the time in that pre-2022 period, such that was the price of the Lucifer rebellion. And those were the tactics to sow division. All of that is behind us now, that is long behind with the Separation Of The Timelines, The Organic Timeline Earth in its own integrity. The AI Artificial Timelines One, having Gone forward and, going off and taking the Lucifer Rebellion with it.

So here we are in 2222, and we're with the, and at the Playa these earth base. And, we want to give you an experience of the Pleiades Earth Base.

Tanaya is the spokesperson for the Pleiadean Earth Base, and will be guiding us today. Thank you then. Tanaya, welcome.

TANAYA PLEIADES EARTH BASE SPOKESPERSON: Welcome everyone. We're very glad to have you here. We should say that in 2010, in January 2010, when the Regional Galactic Governance Council took its emergency vote for the first time to intervene with this advanced technology to stabilize the Ecology Of The Earth, there was a Critical Situation On The Earth. The Ecology Of The Earth was severely in imbalance with Nuclear Factors from Fukushima, with Industrial Factors, With Oceanic Factors, with Landmass Factors, with Forest Factors, with Inner Earth Factors, with Human Density Factors, with Weather Warfare Factors with Electronic Warfare Factors with Scalar Warfare Factors with HAARP Warfare Factors.

And the Regional Galactic Governance Council had to intervene. Otherwise the Luciferian Agenda and Rebellion would have imploded Planet Earth as Tiamat imploded earlier 750,000 years ago.

Tiamat's implosion was a nuclear technology. Earth would have imploded of an Environmental War of a wide variety of technology and would have taken with it many countless billions of souls with no immediate other station for repeat incarnation and would have countermanded the Incarnation Of The Paradise Son of God, incarnation in zero AD with his Crucifixion And Resurrection.

So those were the stakes behind our vote to intervene in January of 2010, which we did and which we followed up with our Overflight over New York on October 13th, 2010, the day before the UN Outer Space Conference meeting at the United Nations Headquarters in New York, on the Protocol For Greeting Extraterrestrials.

Our presence as the Regional Galactic Governance Council over these past million years has been both Arms-Length and Oversight Governance, following the Law Of Non-Interference, and careful High-Technology Monitoring Of A Life Implantation Planet.

As those of you who follow these matters closely, Earth is one of the many of the contiguous 32 life-bearing planets that are Life-Implantation Planets. The Spiritual Dimensions, The Intelligent Civilizations Of Souls, The Spiritual Beings, The Source Itself, have longstanding powers and protocols for developing solar systems of Intelligent Life-Implantation Planets and bring them up developing new species, on entire planets.

This is how life is implanted and developed. And new species are developed from planet to planet.

The Intelligent Design behind Life Implantation is part of the laws of nature. And it's part of the Intelligent Design and is part of Intelligent Life Implantation all at once. So.

The duties of the intelligent civilization of Souls And Spiritual Beings From The Spiritual Dimensions and their opportunities include not only incarnating in the universes of time, space, energy, and matter, so as to evolve their souls. They include creating and maintaining the universes of the multi-verse creating and maintaining the solar systems of galaxies, the planets.

And in this case Earth and the 32 Planets that were subjected to the Rebellion of the Fallen Angels from the Spiritual Dimensions, is an extremely serious event that occurred.

It fell to the Regional Galactic Governance Council who for a million years had been overseeing this area. It fell to us to limit the damage because we are the fallback system inside the universe Uversa of Time, Space, Energy, And Matter.

Think about it. We have the oversight over this area of 32 contiguous planets, where the rebellion occurred for ¾ of a million years. And when did the initial war between the reptilians, the Solar System War with the humans that resulted in the destruction of Tiamat into the Asteroid Belt, the destruction of Mars into an obloid planet, 2 billion souls, having to be transferred from what was Tiamat over to Earth to incarnate? That was 750,000 years ago, that was under our watch!

Our Regional Galactic Governance Council has had to be on alert, Universal Alert, not only for the last 750,000 years, but for the Last Million Years ever since we came together, We have been under High Alert.

This is a Free Will Universe. It's a Freewill Sector Of The Universe.

And the Downside Of Free Will Is Always Ego.

So, we have had to deal intimately with the Human Diaspora, from the Reptilian Human Wars in our Universe Uversa because they have continued Reptilian Human Wars as occurred in the Sol Solar System 750,000 years ago.

The most egregious Planetary wars destroyed planet Tiamat into the Asteroid Belt, destroying the Incarnation Platform for 2 billion human souls, forcing their evacuation after they're painfully being stuck in the Astro for a hundred thousand years. Now these 2 billion Tiamat human souls doing what we could call Rest And Recuperation Incarnation On The Earth.

We have been monitoring them under high alert. Our Regional Galactic Governance Council had been monitoring under high alert from 750,000 years ago on the Sol solar system with Mars now a pumpkin planet with no atmosphere, no surface vegetation, reptilian dinosaurs on the surface and its human population of 1 million underground.

Still, now having to take on those extra 2 Billion souls as an Incarnation Platform, a hundred thousand years after the 750,000 year of war. There is Turbulence at the Incarnation Level, as well as at the Solar System Level.

And in the Spiritual Dimensions, we have High Spiritual Beings, who have choices. They can either monitor this and selflessly be part of the Universe Administration for the benefit of the divine, or they can fester and say, I can do this better than the divine.

And so inside Paradise, we had a group of Spiritual Beings that gradually began to fester with inside the Spiritual Dimensions. They could do this better than the Divine They could do and deal with this sector of the Uversa Universe, with The Tiamat War, destruction of Tiamat and Mars, with the Transfer Of The Human Souls, a hundred thousand years later, with all of the tensions in the 32 contiguous planets that had been left.

All of this time, tensions remained. And we at the Regional Galactic Governance Council, the Pleiades, the Alpha Centaurus, the Sirians, and others who were Advanced Human Civilizations were holding our own.

About 250,000 years ago, the Lucifer, Satan, Caligastia celestial personalities who could maneuver from the spiritual dimensions down into the Uversa universe, into their regions, the regions of the 32 contiguous planets, made their moves.

And by sowing a lot of confusion, including masquerading as Pleiadeans, stating that, the Pleiades had made this this channeling as Pleiadeans, that's where all that comes from causing a huge confusion, starting the Lucifer Rebellion.

And, you know well all of the tragedy that occurred there right up to the Modern Era, when in 1942, the Third Reich came in and attacked and sent a Rip in the Time-Space Fabric Of Earth backwards to 1744, allowing 10,000 Archonic souls Into Earth.

These Archonic souls incarnated as the leadership sector in the modern era, in government finance, science, military, religion, media, and took over the modern media, took over the modern era and oppressed humans with a program of War Disease, Crime, And Poverty.

Attempting to counter the strategic Incarnation In Year Zero Of The Paradise Son of God, who decided to put an end to the Lucifer rebellion by Incarnating On Earth, the second worst of the 32 planets in the Lucifer Rebellion zone and claiming back the entire infrastructure vibration.

And then, continuing skirmishes to April to June, 1982, the False Flag Thule Falklands war in which an AI Artificial Intelligence was released into Earth's environment as a final attempt by the Lucifer rebellion to use Time, the Chronogarchy to destroy Earth and destroy these 32 targeted Life Implantation Planets.

Finally, in 2022, the publication of the Chronogarchy book, and the materialization of the Time in separation of the two Timelines in which, the AI Artificial Timeline One materialized and in effect the AI and all of the AI Entrained souls went into that timeline and disappeared.

And the Organic Timeline that we're on now went into the Fifth Density on, into traveling toward the Sixth Density, which the Pleiades have been on, and which Earth was on prior to the Reptilian Attacks and Reptilian Wars and the Lucifer Rebellion.

So that's kind of a Big Picture of our relationship. We'd been on duty for the last million years, and we've been on alert for the last million years, and it was super alert for the last 750,000 years. Collectively, there has not been like a little bit of relaxation in this sector and it comes down to Free Will.

We can, now at 2222, which is the 200th anniversary of the Separation Of The Timelines, just to mark it in some sort of external marker, the 200th anniversary of the publication of the Chronogarchy book, Earth is beginning to restore itself back into its Upper Dimensional being as moving up into 5D Fifth Dimension, New Earth Toward a Sixth Dimension Stabilization.

You can see what cost it was, what the cost is of three or four or a half-a-dozen Entities, High Angels that were Holographic Fragments Of Source who have their own free will decided to sabotage that Divine Plan.

Look at the pain and destruction that has occurred in this sector of the universe over the last 750,000 years.

Because of this Ego, look at that.

It is something that is an object of contemplation for myself, unendingly. I chose this diplomatic duty with the Regional Galactic Governance Council as part of the Earth Base of the Pleiades.

I could have chosen in our real life in the Pleiades, but I chose this for my own personal Awakeness and growth to try and comprehend — Why this? The Why-ness of wanton destruction, The Wantonness Of Evil.

And there seems to be some sort of Counterpoint between Free Will and Evil, a linguistically in English, at least they seem to rotate around each other Evil and Free Will. They're like the flip side of each other, if you violate and abuse Free Will, the result is Evil.

That seems very simplistic, but it appears to be what occurred in the case of Lucifer Rebellion on Earth and the 32 contiguous Life-Implantation Planets that now 750,000 years and a million years later, we are struggling to recover.

One can get into the rhetoric of, oh look, all these technologies are being released and humanity now has the benefit of all these technologies.

And we're now back up at 5D and it's the New Earth. It looks beautiful, and let's get into that. And that is a perspective to have. And, I have my Cheering Section Presentation as well.

However, there was something in today's presentation that struck me and that I thought I would share with you out beyond all the released technologies and all the fancy things. And that is that of the million years that the Regional Galactic Governance

Council has been in oversight position of earth and its 32 contiguous Life-Implantation Planets, three-quarters of that 750,000 years fully have been in oversight of Sol Solar System and planetary and spiritual Rebellious War and Destruction because it was the Seeds of the Lucifer rebellion that led to the destruction of Tiamat and it's turning into the Asteroid Belt. That was part of the AI Artificial Intelligence, Reptilian Timeline, which is engendered by the precursors of the Lucifer Rebellion.

This takes up practically the entire million years that we at the Pleiades have been on duty.

It is only now after the Separation Of The Timelines in 2022, and fully at the 200th anniversary of the publication of the Chronogarchy book, the 200th anniversary of the separation of the timelines, the establishment of the Pleiades bases on Earth, here in South America.

Our Pleiades Base is in what was South America prior to the Planetary Axis Shift Earth had because of the Timeline Separation.

Earth's Organic Timeline is a long time Vindication of Divine Oriented Souls, a long time Vindication, of Free Will, a long time Vindication of the Divine Love.

And I leave you today with these thoughts. Thank you.

2522 500th Anniversary Of The Separation Of The Organic Earth Timeline And The AI Artificial Intelligence Archonic Timeline. With The 6th Density 6D Andromeda Council Base On Earth

2522 NARRATION: This is the timeline, 2522, the 500th anniversary of the Separation Of The Organic Earth Timeline and the AI Artificial Intelligence Archonic Timeline. We are with the Sixth Density, 6D Andromeda Council Base on Earth.

And welcome. We are now with the spokesperson of the Andromeda Council. Who's actually the successor to a remarkable person who was the Ambassador of the Andromeda Council on Earth.

Zofyo Arni also was the author of the Chronogarchy book. And as we know, Representative Of Earth To The Regional Galactic Governance Council prior to AD 2022 with the Separation Of The Timelines. There is a remarkable, synchronicity here, even though the Andromeda Council was not formally part of the Regional Galactic Governance Council and did not share that close Galactic Husbandry Role Oversight Role with the Regional Galactic Governance Council And Earth during its very perilous period leading up to the Default Of The Spiritual Dimension, Leadership that was in charge of this Region And the Uversa Universe.

We were very lucky to have the Regional Galactic Governance Council, the Alpha Centaurians, the Sirians, the Pleiadeans, and to have personages such as Zofyo Arni in place at that time to bring her through and needless to say the centerpiece of it all, which kept, I would say, the plan of the rebellion, which was really to attempt to, in the latter part of the Rebellion, they knew that this would have in fact destroyed and made a void of a large part of the universe Uversa, you've heard. So, there could have been a runaway effect. We don't know of the black hole created by the implosion of Life-Implantation Planets.

Happily, here we are. And the Andromeda council as a Sixth Density Council has always played an important role on Earth on maintaining a High Frequency and on bringing Love, Light, And Life, which are the three significant Dimensions of a Six Density Civilization.

We're very happy to have the successor of Zofyo Arni here as, the Ambassador from the Andromeda Council to Earth to represent us today and to bring us an update, Ambassador over to you.

ANDROMEDA COUNCIL AMBASSADOR TO EARTH TIMELINE ZERO: Well, Thank You. Yes. The Andromeda Council made an independent decision independently of the Regional Galactic Governance Council, which was primarily a Governance Oversight Role over the last million plus years in this region of the Uversa universe.

And it was a very important one because the Regional Galactic Governance Council were the backstop to the tremendous hazard, an impact that the Default In The Spiritual Dimensions took place. And we're very grateful for, the role that they played and not only that for the role that the Earth Representatives And Earth itself that, came together.

And in 2022, there was the manifestation of the Two Timelines, The Organic Earth Timeline And The AI Artificial Timelines.

Souls On Earth had opted one way or the other. And Earth was once again restored on its Divine Blueprint and, basically, the legacy of Exopolitics in the Exopolitics book and the Exopolitics movement, which first appeared in the year 2000, by Zofyo Arni was very important followed by the Omniverse Trilogy that appeared first in 2014.

And then in the subsequent years, because that really restored the knowledge of the Scientific Basis Of The Spiritual Dimensions that had been obscured by the religions, which were the Luciferian substitute for the Spiritual Sciences that the Spiritual Dimension representatives were to have engendered on the 32 Life-Implantation Planets.

So that was very important as well. And then of course, the Chronogarchy book really exposed and accelerated the Separation Of The Timelines because it exposed Time As The Control Weapon and Dimension by which the defaulted spiritual beings of the Spiritual Dimensions were able to capture souls, and how the Sentient AI Artificial Intelligence was able to capture souls.

All of this is very important and, and we are very grateful. We at the Andromeda Council are very grateful to the People Of Earth, to the People Of The 32 Continuous Planets that put up a tremendous Resistance that brought together a Critical Mass by 2022, that Materialized The Organic Timeline. We are grateful to the Regional Galactic Governance Council and its members for being the essential backstop for the Spiritual Dimensions In This Sector Of The Universe. Who knows if they had defaulted as well, if this had not spread throughout, the neighboring galaxies, like the Andromeda Galaxy.

So, our role really as a Council, a Galactic Council in a neighboring Galaxy, that is at an Upper Dimensional Human Civilization averaging in a Sixth Density. Some of our civilizations are at the Upper Dimension, Seventh, Eighth, Ninth Density. Their role is to provide liaison and background to Life-Implantation Planets Like Earth in the Milky Way Galaxy that have undergone significant challenge, with the Default Of Their

Celestial Personalities and Spiritual Dimension Leadership like the Lucifer Rebellion.

And as I understand it, that is the focus of your series of Broadcasts, that we in the Andromeda Council have been rebroadcasting throughout the Andromeda galaxy, because this has been a real event, this is affected not only Earth and the contiguous planets of the Lucifer Rebellion in the Milky way Galaxy. This has affected the Andromeda Galaxy as well, even though we're at Sixth Density and above.

The Density we symbolize are the Dimensions of Love, Light, And Life, and those are Dimensions which deeply reflect Source and what Earthlings, have come over the Eras to call God.

However, we know from the Science that it is the Collective Spiritual Dimension itself, including the Intelligent Civilization Of Souls, all of the Spiritual Beings, And Source Itself, Collectively that carries out the functions of Source and, creates and maintains all of the Universes Of Time, Energy, Space, And Matter.

In our roles as Spiritual Dimension Souls, we at the Andromeda Galaxy and we in the Andromeda Council have in part a function of Deity in maintaining and creating the Planets of, and the Universes of the Multi-verse. We help create and maintain all of the Life-Implantation Planets and Incarnation Planets in the Milky Way Galaxy including the 32 affected life-implantation planets that were affected by the Lucifer rebellion.

And we know, your Scientists have now calculated — I want to reiterate that they knew this — and this was broadcast through the Omniverse Trilogy. The knowledge of the Omniverse was first published in 2014 on Planet Earth through Zofyo Arni's Omniverse Trilogy books that the numbers of universes in the Multiverse was estimated at 10 to the 7th to the 7th.

And that is a humongously large number in the words of the Stanford University discoverers. There's no, word in earthly languages, for that number.

If you write that out by hand, or in 12-point type, that number would be more than 260 million miles long. That is, quite a feat of Universe Understanding that the Third Density Earth by 2014, as it was nearing, it's moving into, and it was actually along the Organic, Divine Timeline, and was able to share all of that through replicable Science.

And that is the function that we at the Andromeda Council have on Earth and the 32 contiguous planets in the Milky Way Galaxy. we have really brought a feeling of, as I said, the higher Dimensions of Love, Light, Life, And Truth. And these are the divine attributes that you will find the Sixth Density, the Eighth Density, the Ninth Density, which is the density of the Life-Bearing Planets, and Civilizations that you will find in the Andromeda Galaxy, and that are members of the Andromeda Council.

We have kept that kind of a background liaison with the Earth over time while our Collegial Governance Council, the Regional Galactic Governance Council — the Pleiadeans, Alpha Centaurians, and Sirians have been more, hands-on governance concerned about the maintenance of governance here, ensuring that even though some horrific things that happened, for example, when the Third Reich intervened in 1942 and created, through its use of Advanced Energy Weapons they had obtained from the Reptilians in their Space program, a Rip in Earth's Time-Space Fabric back to 1744, such that 10,000 Archonic souls entered at that point, for yet another assault by the Lucifer Rebellion. That is the sort of Urgency that the Regional Galactic Governance Council would take immediate and Urgent Oversight over.

I'll think that though we were in the background, maintaining the Love, maintaining the Life and Light, maintaining the Truth, maintaining the Wisdom, which is those are the Dimensions, which, Sixth, Seventh, Eighth, And Ninth Density embody. At the Third Density, the dimensions that are embodied are Time And Space.

And those are the densities that your reality experiences, are most concerned with. And that's why Duality Consciousness — I Win You Lose — in these 3D battles really emerges. Whereas, in in our realities, we are in the areas of Love, Life, Light,

Truth, and, those are the Divine Values. We are focused on maintaining those High Values in the background, not only for the Andromeda Counsel, but for the Uversa Universe as a whole, and for our neighboring Milky Way Galaxy that has gone through many challenges.

We have not had a Spiritual Dimension Default in the Andromeda Council, like there was in the Milky Way Galaxy. We were able to identify and to work with an outstanding Earthling individual. Zofyo Arni then the author of Exopolitics, the author of the Omniverse trilogy, and who brought that knowledge back the Lucifer rebellion. Who had published the Chronogarchy book in 2022.

His birth had been strategically planned in 1942. At the time of the Third Reich counter attack with the Rip in the Fabric Of Time-Space going back to 1744, his Presence would have come in to the Earth Fabric, to hold everything together. And, he brought that famous phrase in 1942, Praise The Lord And Pass The Ammunition.

He brought the Vibration Of The Paradise Son Of God, very much in mind, to those forces that understood that with the Third Reich, they were dealing with this fear of a Strike directly from the Luciferian Forces to attempt, once again, to destroy 32 contiguous Life-Implantation Planets with a view toward the striking or bringing down the Milky Way Galaxy.

And with that, to destroying, as much as possible of Uversa, our Universe, and Creation, as much as possible by that time, the amnesty of Lucifer and his lieutenants, Satan, Caligastia, and others in this mass had congealed into Evil.

We've done the analysis that the two Counterpoint are Free Will and Evil. These are counterpoints even in the English language. Our focus as the Andromeda Council has always been to maintain the Highest Frequency Possible.

We saw that Earth Lane, that Special Earth Link at the time of the latter stages of the Lucifer Rebellion at the time of the Exopolitics Movement. Once the Exopolitics book had been published in the year 2000. Once, he was involved in publishing the three Omniverse books and in bringing together and publishing all of the Chronogarchy books, he needed our support. Because that was the time in which, all of the Fake And False, Fake And False, I would say Upper Dimensional Human Civilizations Channelings would appear, the Fake Pleiadeans who, really would appear to try and Block The Mission, the Organic Earth Timeline Mission, and would appear to try and implement the Luciferian mission in a very sharp way.

That's why we came forward and publicly appointed Zofyo Arni Earth Representative Of The Andromeda Council to provide on Earth, to provide a Counterweight, and, to try and allay some of the confusion that was there.

Zofyo Arni performed very well historically. His contributions with the Exopolitics books, the three Omniverse books and the Chronogarchy books, I think stand on their own as well as his contributions as a *persona*, as a Tribunal Of Conscience Judge dispensing, Natural And Common Law Justice at that time in many venues in Tribunals.

We just want to express our Sixth, Seventh, Eighth, And Ninth Density Appreciation for that Contribution, at this time.

This is a time where we can begin to Celebrate and we can begin to, Share The Profound Joy Of Contemplation in the Dimensions of Love, Life, Light, and Truth, which are the Sixth, Seventh, and Eighth, Ninth Density Dimensions.

These are the Dimensions that the Andromeda Galaxy, the Andromeda council is charged with anchoring and representing here in the Milky Way Galaxy in its representation on Earth, And In the 32 Contiguous Life-Implantation Planets. That is what we try to bring and to offer a Mirror and a Source of those Vibrations of Love, those Observations Of Life, Light and of Truth. Because for so many centuries and even millennia, the Divine Essence of Love, Life, Light, and Truth had been drained and blocked from Earth, and from the 32 contiguous planets by the conscious default of the Spiritual Dimension Leaders here.

It is a truism, an Absolute Truth that God Is Love. Love is a Dimension that is Inherent In Source.

God Is Love. Love Is God And Emanates God. God Loves And Emanates Love As Source.

Anything that is less than the Vibration Of Love is less than the Vibration Of The Divine Source since Source Is Love.

And God Is One Is Male-Female.

Is Beyond Dualities.

And that is the Realization that we at The Reality That Source God Is One is what we of The Andromeda Council at 6, 7, 8, 9 Density are here to Ground and Reflect here at Earth and at the Life-Bearing Planets that have experience so much of Separation and Fragmentation of Everything Except Oneness.

The Oneness Of God Is Love Is One Is Truth Is Life Is Light. Lucifer means light bearer, and it was through light and time that Lucifer was able to cause confusion.

And that's why in the run-up to the materialization of the split of the timelines into Timeline Zero Organic Divine Love, Truth Timeline, and AI Artificial Intelligence Timeline, the Oneness, The Love, The Life, The Truth Of The Divine Timeline In Vibration is Crucial.

And why the Souls Who Identified As Divine knew the Critical Mass and the AI entrained souls were magnetized into the AI timeline.

And the Lucifer Rebellion was siphoned off into AI and ended on the same year as the publication of the Chronogarchy book, exposing Time. As the Andromeda Council is to Embody the Sixth, Seventh, Eighth, Ninth Densities here on Earth's Organic Timeline Of Love, Life, Truth, and Light. For the Milky Way Galaxy in conjunction with the Regional Galactic Governance Council for the 32 Contiguous Life-Implantation Planets and for Earth Destination Planet Of The Paradise Son of God Creator Bottom Line Of The Universe, a Universe within which the Andromeda Galaxy sits.

We stand on these Pillars. We stand on the Pillar of Source, God, Love Life, Truth, Light. We stand on the Pillar of Paradise

Son of God, Incarnating on Earth in the context as told by the Epochal Revelation in 1955 of Earth, Urantia book.

Earth is a Bestowal Planet.

There is no doubt about it. And that's why we have the Andromeda Council here from a neighboring galaxy And the Urantia book Epochal Revelation as updated explicitly in the run-up to the separation of the Divine Earth Organic Timeline in 2022. The Explicit Update Of The Epochal Revelation, which was the Exopolitics book, the Omniverse Trilogy, and the Chronogarchy books.

Update brought into being by Zofyo Arni.

The Andromeda Council are here always for you as a Materialization of Source of God on Earth.

Thank you.

2122: Short Grey ET Base On Zero Earth Timeline And In Grey ET Space Station Above Earth In Continuing Grey ET Soul Development Mission To Earth Agondonters

2122 NARRATION: Timeline 2122 and we're at the Short Grey ET Earth Base and Space Station Spaceship, Grey Earth, Zero Timeline in the soul development Agondonter mission of the Short Greys that has always been the Short Grey Mission To Earth that has been longstanding.

The Short Grey's mission here on Earth and throughout the Universe To Timeline Zero, the Divine Oriented Timeline has been Soul Development. We call it the Hybrid Grey Human Soul. And, we have substantiated case reports that were reported by Cyan Briden, from New Zealand, Exopolitics, Zealand UFO, having gone up as a young girl into the Short Grey Spaceship, having been being up and playing there with Human Souls, including the Soul Of Her Future Son, which she met there and then fast forward, and she was married and pregnant. She was Beamed Up.

At the appropriate time, the Case Studies say, that usually the Human Soul in the usual case of a human, at about three months teleports from the Portal In The Spiritual Dimension, right up against the womb of the pregnant mother with the fetus and then embeds itself in the fetus. And that's what Cyan Briden reports that there was a special operation performed on the Grey ET Ship. On the Grey ET Hybrid Soul Mission Ship, where a Special Grey came on board and embedded the Soul Of Her Son that she had met before on the Grey ET Ship into her womb.

These Grey ET Ships, in fact are part of the Short Grey ET Hybrid Soul Development Mission. We say Hybrid because the Souls that the Grey ETs are developing — our Hybrid Human Grey ET Souls — the issue is whether many of the Human Beings along the Earth Timeline that we have been discussing, that were in Resistance to the Lucifer rebellion and played crucial roles along that Lucifer rebellion were the product of Grey ET Hybrid Soul Development Mission. Because it could have been that the Earth Human Soul on its own, was not highly developed enough or strong enough to have resisted the onslaught of the Lucifer Rebellion.

Look at all of its stages, going back, initially three quarters of a million years with the Solar System War, with the Reptilian Invasion Of The Sol Solar System, the implosion of Tiamat into the Asteroid Belt, the imprisonment as it were, of 2 billion Humans Souls from Tiamat in the Astral, then the incarnation of those Human Souls On Earth, the flattening of Mars into an obloid planet with little atmosphere, no surface vegetation and reptilian dinosaurs, carnivorous dinosaurs on the surface with the 1 million human population, Genetic Cousins Of Those On Earth consigned to underground. That was the opening salvo of the Lucifer Rebellion.

That's happened at 750,000 years before 2020, say. The next major Lucifer Rebellion Salvo was in 1942 with the attack of the Third Reich with energy weapons that were supplied by a Reptilian Base On The Earth's Moon. That led to a Rip in the Earth's Time Space Fabric all the way back to 1744, permitting the entry of the 10,000 Archonic souls through that Rip in the Time Space Fabric that brought them into through Retrocausation into the Earth's Leadership, such that Archonic Souls incarnated in all positions of Leadership Over The Community Of Human Souls On Planet Earth. Earth's leaders were what looked like human beings but in fact, were Archonic souls inside human bodies in a concerted effort of War, Disease, Crime And Poverty And Oppression of the Human Community so that All Governments, All Religions, All Science On Military, All Wars, All Levels Of Government, Municipal, Regional, Provincial, State, etc., were in league to oppress the human community.

So were Religions and so was the Interlife, the reincarnation matrix taken over by the Archonic. Spiritual Dimension Entities and so this was an aspect of the Lucifer Rebellion.

Perhaps it was that the Earthing Human Soul, although being called an Agondonter was not of itself sufficiently strong and resistant so as to resist the onslaught of the Lucifer Rebellion. In that sense, the Short Grey ETs either on their own monitoring the situation, or were called in by the Universe Administration. The Grey ETs were called in to start a Soul Hybridization Program because the Short Grey ETs had very strong souls and this way could Hybridize Particular Leadership Souls.

For example, the Soul of Cyan Briden was herself, the Leader of UFO New Zealand, who was in close contact with the Minister of Defence of New Zealand. She actually was instrumental in having the Ministry of Defence and New Zealand do a very early Disclosure much earlier than any other nations. So Cyan Briden is an example of the Grey ET Soul Hybridization.

Another example of the Grey ET Soul Hybridization is Alexander Uine, the US Chrononaut, who would Time Travel from 1971 Project Pegasus back up to the DARPA Forward Time Base in 2045. That US Chrononaut testified that he had numerous interactions with Grey ETs in early childhood of a Dimensional nature and that the Short Greys monitored him throughout his life, including on his Mars Visitations. And he may have been, in fact, given or afforded a Grey ET Hybrid Soul because of his crucial role in Resistance to the Lucifer rebellion, going back and forth along Earth's Timeline Zero for 2045 back to 1971.

That Timeline was still in open warfare in that Lucifer Rebellion Planetary Warfare, prior to the 1982 attempt to release onto the planet of the AI Plasma-Base Artificial Intelligence in the Thule Island, Falkland Islands False Flag War, which the Reptilian British Queen, Margaret Thatcher, and Ronald Reagan, all engaged in on behalf of the Lucifer Rebellion.

Additionally, it is thought that another key individual may have had a hybrid Grey ET Soul — Zofyo Arni, the author of the Exopolitics, Omniverse Trilogy, and Chronogarchy books, because those were so crucial in bringing back key information that had been sequestered by the Lucifer rebellion, and that had been suppressed by Luciferian infiltrators into the Exopolitics and UFO movement. And also, because that individual Zofyo Arni had been tasked with incarnating in that crucial year of 1942, to serve as an Anchor against the 1942 incursion by the Third Reich and subsequent directed energy Rip in the Spacetime Fabric back to 1744 and the incursion of 10,000 Archonic souls.

Individuals like Zofyo Arni, Alexander Uine, and Cyan Briden and others, may have been the sorts of individuals who were brought aboard and involved in the Grey Et Hybrid Grey Human Soul program.

We are sharing this with you now. We have here, an Ambassador from the Grey ET Ship itself who is joining us at the Grey ET base which is in the former Arctic Circle, Prior To The Timeline Separation Earth Axis Shift Of Planet Earth. Ambassador, Welcome. What do you say of the speculation we've been making?

SHORT GREY ET AMBASSADOR TO EARTH TIMELINE ZERO: Yes, thank you very much. I'm very happy to be here with you today are speaking to you through a special machine, whereby my Telepathy is translated into whatever Earth language you are listening to. If you are English speaking, you'll be hearing this in English. You're Russian speaking, you'll be hearing this in Russian. And of course, if you're a Telepath, you'll be listening to this in

Telepathy because now on the organic timeline of New Earth, it is almost a Majority Telepathic Population, although not totally.

And New Earth Zero now is a period of transition. But our technology is doing very useful things like Voice To Telepathy To Print and things like that.

That was the very artful explanation that you gave. And yes, there's a lot of truth in in what you said. And our Mission Of Soul Development has been to Supplement The Planetary Defenses and the Human Community of Agondonter souls with Human Grey Hybrid Souls that could withstand an invasion such as the Lucifer Rebellion engendered, and that included a Reptilian invasion and Sentient Artificial Intelligence invasion and the invasion of the Orion greys.

There are over 250 distinct species of Grey ETs that have been Exopolitically identified. Our Species Of Greys has a certain Evolutionary History. We value our Soul and our God Connection, our Connection To Source, A Paradise Connection To Source most strongly. That is why we forsake the Animal Incarnation Cycle because we at some point, we become involved in some fairly severe conflicts both in the Spiritual Dimension Level and in the Universal Level here in the Uversa Universe.

These were part of the Antecedents of the Lucifer Rebellion. And we saw that our best strategy was to focus our energies on our Connection To Source and on the fortification of our Holographic Fragments Of Source which are our Divine Soul. And we transferred as much of our Divine Soul from the Spiritual Dimensions where most souls are anchored during an incarnation cycle. In a Reincarnation Cycle, let's say that up to 70 percent of the soul will be anchored in your Spiritual Dimension and then 30% or so remaining to 50% may be incarnating in One To Three Simultaneous Incarnations in one or more Universes.

That can leave those one to three simultaneous incarnations in various universe contexts in Exophenotypes be the human, be they avian, or whatever, it can leave them vulnerable, particularly if you're incarnating in a spiritually unstable sector or incarnation.

We were able, we showed the Short Grey ETs we're able to monitor and make a judgement that in particular, we foresaw that the antecedents of the Lucifer Rebellion within the spiritual dimensions, within paradise, were going to overwhelm the paradise circuits, were going to overwhelm the universe, and its universe circuits, and possibly other universe circuits.

Therefore, we made a Species Judgment to Forego Incarnation in an Exophenotype, that is in an animal format, like a human mammal. And to come directly into a Grey format, which has the Minimal Animal Genetic Interface and Slow Down from a Soul Development Point Of View. We decided as a species and to specialize in Soul Hybrid Soul Development with other incarnating souls such as to Fortify The Various Human Souls.

In those Solar Systems And Galaxies And Universes that we foresaw through our monitoring system, we're going to be Targeted By Those Spiritual Dimension, Spiritual Beings Personalities, on the edge of going into Abuse Of Freewill and breaking off to going Into Diabolical Or Evil Open Breaking With The Godhead. All of this proceeds from Abuse Of Freewill. It's very simple, Ego-based.

That was a commitment that we the Short Greys made. And we contributed space specifically for the Lucifer rebellion on Earth, and in the 32 contiguous life-implantation planets that were the target of the Lucifer rebellion. Here in this area of the Milky Way galaxy. And that were impacted as was Earth there was one planet that was even more impacted than Earth. However, we focus on Earth Because Earth Was Bestowal Planet A Paradise Son of God chose Earth for his or her one physical incarnation in its creation of a universe, and that's what occurred.

We deployed ourselves around this area, around the same time as the Regional Galactic Governance Council, but even longer, because our perspective is a long one. We have been in operation for Five To 10 Million Years in the Milky Way Galaxy, and in other galaxies at life-implantation planets. And our mission is to foster Human Grey Hybrid Souls, especially in the

Lower Densities In The Third Densities, especially in planets that have fallen from Upper Densities From Seventh Eighth Ninth Densities, And They've Had The Falls And Fallen Down Into Third Density.

Some have fallen even down into Second And Become Insect Planets Or Dinosaur Planets And Have To Build Themselves That Back Up.

And it's there that our specialized teams come in, because we produce those specialized very Strong Souls that are able to come in for specialized missions, like Cyan Briden in New Zealand, who was able to work and take up the original tasks that the Maori brought. Remember, New Zealand was pristine, and then the Maori arrived there, from Tahiti until the Reptilian Kings And Queens of England brought their Captain Cook, to bring down the Maori. And now that there's of course, that revival of the Maori up, and then we brought in a series of our souls, Short Grey Souls into New Zealand.

An example of a New Zealand Short Grey Hybrid Human Soul is Cyan Briden, who was able to come aboard our Ship as a child and acquire a Hybrid Grey Human Soul herself, and then meet and play with the Soul Of Her Son, as a child on our Great ET Ship that orbits over Earth. Then, at the appropriate time when she was pregnant in the three months period, that around that time was teleported back up into the ship and had an Implantation Procedure Of Her Son's Soul into the fetus.

And Cyan Briden's son went on to be a lawyer and, and a spiritual personage, carrying out many, important duties and keeping the fabric of New Zealand high, which of course by then had been highly targeted by the Reptilian Queen.

They put a reptilian New Zealand Prime Minister close to the Reptilian Queen at the time. It's always been a fight with the Australian and New Zealand Reptilians prior to the Separation Of The Timelines in 2022. We always had a good hand in because of Zofyo Arni who was one of our Hybrid Grey ET Human Souls who came in 1942 and anchored down Earth Timeline Zero

Organic Timeline Zero, so that it was unaffected and was not imploded by the Rip in the Time Space back to 1744. Going forward, with the production of the Exopolitics, the Omniverse Trilogy, the Chronogarchy books was able to acquire that mass of energy, that Critical Mass, that was so important.

That is what occurred along this Timeline. It has been our grey ET Agondonter Souls that we have developed here on the Ships that have really kept the Zero Organic Timeline going.

That is something that people should know, and I'm very glad to provide the context for now. You could ask, Why Are We Still Here? We're still on now into, 2122? Well, we're into 2122, and the Timelines are now a Hundred Years into their Separation.

However, we're here as part of the Mix Of Earth and the Mix Of Earth Contains Humans. It contains a Regional Galactic Governance Council. It's Open Contact now, with many Extraterrestrial Races, all in Positive. We do not have Negative Occupation now.

We're all in a Positive Modality. The Negative Occupation was an Artifact of the Lucifer Rebellion. It was not inherent in how things are in Uversa Universe. It was an artifact of Lucifer rebellion. When the Timeline Separated, at 2022 and the AI And Those Entities And Humans And Others That Were Identified With Lucifer Rebellion Went Off On Their Artificial Intelligence Timeline One, well, all of the Positive Aspects Who Were Part Of The Singularity Of The New Earth Are Part Of The Singularity Of The New Earth.

The Short Greys Are Earthlings, as now the Regional Galactic Governance Council, Pleiadeans who are here as the Earth Base, the Alpha Centaurians, the Syrians, the others who are here as far as their Earth Bases. We Are All Earthlings now. This is what it means to be on Earth, and as well as the humans and as well as many others. This Is A Hybrid Planet, and this is a Hybrid Universe, and it is a Freewill Universe.

However, it is a Freewill Universe Based On Divine Law. Free Will does not carry with it the ability to break Universal And

Divine Law without consequences. That is the conceit of Lucifer Rebellion or any rebellion by any Cosmic Criminal.

We are very fulfilled by our Deployment in this sector of Uversa over the last several million years, because organically, we understood what was occurring in the Spiritual Dimensions among Spiritual Beings among the Intelligent Civilization Of Souls.

As far as the Abuse Of Freewill, we held many meetings amongst ourselves and debated issues. We made a collective decision to forgo Incarnation Into Exophenotypes, and decided to become, specialized as beings that focused on their Divine Souls in the most efficient way to do that was as a short reign in the universes of time, energy space and matter.

And this was our commitment and how we saw we could keep Soul Development In The Universities Of Time, Energy Space, And Matter reinforced now. Because we don't look like humans caused a lot of confusion and that is something that widely, you know, has had repercussions up and down the line.

At the same time, there's been a lot of appreciation of us. If you go into some of the places, for example, just prior to 2022 and the Split Of The Timelines, around our Positive Role, The Positive Role Of The Short Greys In Soul Development.

And so, even at the time prior to the formal separation of the timelines, our role was studied, within the Exopolitical framework.

If you go back to the Chronogarchy book itself by Zofyo Arni, you will notice that, there's at least one chapter there, which deals with the positive ET adduction of Zofyo Arni and the US Chrononaut Alexander Uine tonight by the advanced ETs, along with a US President prior to his Presidency and speculates that it was the Short Greys that did this, and elevated the President's Soul to Hybrid Human Soul to become a non-Reptilian President.

There's a chapter in the Chronogarchy book that addresses this that I would like to draw your attention to. These are very deep matters and that believe me, we're part of your Earthly Equation. We continue to create and train Hybrid Humans

Short Grey ET Souls, embedded into the fetus born to human mothers on a systematic basis that keep the leavening of the Soul Population On The New Earth and, you know, keeps it Growing At High And Connected To A Source Because Our Soul Population Is As Diverse As Our Genetic Population.

And the Universes, don't forget, are Designed to be Machines for Soul Development. We are part of the team in the Universes that focuses on Soul Development, and we are very content in our work it's fulfilling work.

We're very glad to have presented this to you so that you have a fuller picture of how this works. And, you have a fuller picture of the strain on the Soul And Universe Development System that events like a Default Of Spiritual Beings In The Spiritual Dimension and, a Default Of Celestial Personalities, how that really is Very Serious.

And that's the Default Of Free Will. Well, so that's a risk that the designers of Creation Source And The Spiritual Dimension take. Now there's a review to see, well, Have We Gone Too Far With Free Will? Well, what were the flaws there? And like anything else, like any creation, there's always a review, continuous quality improvement in Universe Creation, all of that is improving.

And we're very happy, to have been able to share this Perspective with you. As I understand it, this Broadcast is, being broadcast up and down the Earth's Organic Timeline, up to, 2522, the 500th anniversary and beyond and down past 1942, past 1744 down passed into the Times for those who have Ears To Hear And Eyes To See and whatever mechanism there is there, to pick it out so that, we preserve the Integrity Of The Earth's Zero Timeline and our Grey ET Role in it, which I believe has been so worthwhile.

And I want to thank you for coming here today. And, I'm now ready for your questions. Thank you.

TIMELINE:

2022 With Zofyo Arni On The Chronogarchy Book Timeline At The Critical Mass Separation Of The Zero Organic Earth Timeline And The AI Artificial Timeline One For AI Entrained Soulless Humans

We are at 2022 with Zofyo Arni on the Chronogarchy book Timeline at the Critical Mass Separation of the Zero, Organic Earth Timeline and the AI Artificial Timeline One for AI Entrained, Soulless Humans. This is what you would really call Ground Zero for the New Earth the Organic Timeline and of course Ground Zero for the AI Timeline One, the offshoot into AI Entrained Humans and the Abuse Of Freewill.

We're here with Zofyo Arni who in a way has served as Midwife to this moment. Zofyo, would you like to take over the helm at this point?

ZOFYO ARNI AT 2022 ON THE SEPARATION OF THE EARTH TIMELINES ZERO AND ONE: Thank you. Thank you very much. And thank you for having us brought through this Timeline Journey through this Chronogarchy, and Chronogarchy Challenge up to this moment. This is a very powerful and emotional moment for all of us.

The realization that the Earth as we know it is in fact becoming More Real, and the Earth as we know it is Disappearing. Simultaneously, it's what an art we call the *chiaroscuro* moment, Shadow And Light, Light Within Shadow.

Those of us who were battling the Lucifer Rebellion all these Millennia we're committed to the Timeline Zero Earth as we experienced Earth. Saving what we experienced until that moment, when the Critical Mass became too strong such that Good And Evil could no longer coexist as One. That had to break into Artificial Intelligence that had Abused Free Will, and had Channeled Divine Freewill too long.

That is what the Essence I think has come down to in this moment in 2022 when the Chronogarchy book has been published when the Chronogarchy Challenge has been exposed for all to see and everything is transparent.

Freewill has been challenged too deeply for a single Timeline to continue on One Holographic Reality that we call Earth. That Earth has to Bifurcate Into Two.

I can recall that back in June of 1982, as we were preparing for the Second Special Session On Disarmament at the United Nations in June 1982, we were organizing a Peace Concert called PeaceQuake on the San Francisco Civic Center Plaza.

And after we did the Peace Concert, which incidentally, Pete Wozniak the cofounder of Apple, cut a check for the expenses, we went out to Marin County and went up a Mountain and there was a lady psychic there who said to us, "The Earth will be divided and all the Generals that do War will go on to that Earth". That Earth is the Earth Timeline One of the AI Artificial Intelligence with its policy of War, Disease, Crime And Poverty, which is not a Human Divine Soul Policy.

Quite the opposite. You had to sell War, Disease, Crime, and Poverty through Propaganda, Patriotism Fear, Duality Consciousness of I win-you lose. It was no way thought to be sold after Critical Mass on each of the Timelines was reached so that the Two Timelines Materialized visibly that they could no longer share a Single Holographic Earth. The two Holographic Groups had to split. The two Timelines — one's the AI Timeline and the other is the Organic Zero Timeline, which is the Timeline Of Divine Souls and that is what is occurring in this moment. And I think that is what you the Timeline Narrator have wanted to share with us in this Timeline Tour of the Chronogarchy Challenge that you have been taking us on.

Each of us remembers our Birth and has struggled to go back to remember our Birth. I did it through Rebirthing in Los Angeles in the early 1980s at Mi Casa off of Sunset Boulevard in West Hollywood.

I was called in during the Interlife before Birth after a lot of Free Will Planning because the Forward Time Base at 2045 had mounted a Zero Timeline Alert on the Third Reich. The Third Reich was much more hazardous to Earth than had been generally assumed.

It was not just a moment of Worker Democracy, a Martial Moment of Salutes & Military Order. The Third Reich was a Counter Attack of the defaulted Paradise Spirit Spiritual Dimension Personalities that were coming in again for a Destructive Wave Invasion Of Earth, the Bestowal Planet Of A Paradise Son Of God and of the 32 contiguous Life-Implantation Planets.

The Third Reich already had Working Alliances with the Reptilians with Space Bases on Earth's Moon and Mars. The Third Reich had Reptilian advanced Directed Energy weapons.

The Third Reich was already to move out into the physical universe and to bring down this sector of the galaxy of the Universe Administration, that's what was at stake.

And we should look at through retro-causation which incarnated souls at that time, starting with George HW Bush, starting with all the Wall Street bankers that promoted the Third Reich starting with the Thule Society that promoted the Third Reich throughout Germany. Luciferian Wall Street Bankers promoted Bolshevism at the same time, which is a Luciferian doctrine. So that the same parties were promoting Luciferianism,

Satanism, Bolshevism, and Third Reich Nazism all Aggregations Of Free Will against the Divine, just with different faces.

So, it was at this point that a cadre of us were called up to incarnate in Earth in 1942 and to Anchor In The Spiritual Dimension and to serve as the Line across which the Luciferian Order could not cross.

I was called in to incarnate through the Portal in the Caribbean Sea by what was called the Inner Earth or Atlantis at that point, the US Naval Base at Pensacola, Florida in the year 1942. And I incarnated on a Sunday a few months after a False Flag Pearl Harbor Attack by the Axis forces of this Luciferian Axis Front on the United States. This was a Triple Dimension War, whereby the Freemasons control so much of the Action at a Hidden Level working through the Order of the Garter under the Reptilian Queen, I mean so many levels as always.

In the Earth Mix Zero Timeline I came in on May 24 1942. That was the Global Birthday Of The Super Reptilian Queen, Queen Victoria. And it was also awesome Sunday Our Lady Help of Christians.

So, we were signaling and drawing in on the Vibration United Uniting The Awareness Of The Paradise Son Of God that the Third Reich was an attack by the Defaulted Spiritual Beings. The Fallen Angels the Luciferian souls on the Bestowal Planet of Earth and on the 32 Life-Bearing contiguous planet.

In that year 1942 using Directed Energy Weapons which the Reptilians had developed, and which the Third Reich had obtained through their Reptilian Allies On The Earth Moon Base, they were able to create a rip in the Time Space Fabric pre-arranged such that 10,000 archonic souls were able to teleport into the Incarnation platform of Earth going back to 1744. Thereby by retro-causation, start the Incarnation cycle of the Archonic souls into human bodies and all of the accompanying Archonic reptilian souls that incarnated from 1744 forward in all Leadership Sectors of the Modern Anti-Human, Anti-Christic Earth.

Whereby all Leadership In Education, Science, Health Care, Medicine, Governance, Religions, Science, Military, Intelligence, Media, The Arts all of these were led by Archonic Souls that were cognizant of a Coordinated Plan. Unknown to the billions of human Souls that were incarnating into Human Bodies at the Controlled Level on Earth and thereby Oppressed. In a Planetary Policy known as War, Disease, Crime And Poverty and with an explicit mission of Soul Attrition.

So that the Luciferian mission was The Attrition Of Souls, The Destruction Of Souls The Control of the Organic Zero Earth Timeline, in the Lucifer Rebellion, the spreading of The Abuse Of Free Will, the spreading of the Spiritual Default and The Implosion of the Spiritual Dimension in the Universe, a Default that would eventually spread to the Implosion Of Large Galactic Segments of the Universe, and the Universe Itself, and perhaps of All Creation, Thereby Nullifying Source, Nullifying God.

That was the Explicit Intent.

It was in this backdrop that a Cadre Of Us Hybrid Souls was brought in from the Short, Grey Hybrid Human Soul Ships that were in orbit around Earth in the 1942 time horizon and embedded into the Wombs Of Pregnant Mothers in the circumstances of families that would allow our Maximum Leverage And Life Stories for the Resistance And Overturning of the Lucifer Rebellion during our Lives.

This is how the Short Grey ET Hybrid Human Soul Incarnation works in times of Urgency.

And this was the most Serious Planetary Urgency. It involves Time Travel Retro-Causation going back to 1744, with 10,000 Archonic souls, bringing forward its Archonic human society in the modern Earth Timeline up to 1942 and beyond to the present Era. Ready to come to the Modern Era and impose the New World Order; ready to turn Earth into an Archonic New World Order as of 2022.

And it was only through the Short Grey ET Hybrid Human Soul Incarnations in 1942 that neutralized the Third Reich and anchored and stabilized the Organic Earth Timeline Zero.

Then as Zofyo Arni, my Soul was able to land the return of knowledge of the Organized Universe through the Exopolitics book in the year 2000, and launch the Exopolitics Movement, with the assistance of the 2045 Forward Time Base. The Exopolitics book and awareness was Time Traveled from 2045 back to the 1971 White Hats, who in turn seeded the Exopolitics Movement through retrocausation at the 1983 Conference at College of the Siskiyous, and future Exopolitical events such as the 2001 Disclosure Project Press Conference at which I was a Participant.

As Zofyo Arni, my Soul was able to land the return of replicable Scientific knowledge of the Spiritual Dimensions and of the Omniverse as the third Cosmological body through which humanity understands the Cosmos, through the Omniverse Books Trilogy, starting in 2014.

The publication of the Chronogarchy book named the Chronogarchy and named Time as their destructive Dimension and led to the Manifestation Of The Two Timelines in 2022. Timeline Zero, Organic Earth Timeline and Timeline One the AI Timeline.

The AI Timeline thought that it had become the only Timeline on Earth and that's what its significant contour was in its sort of Final, Last Hurrah, which was the 2019-2020-2021 "PlanDemic".

The 2019-2020-2021 PlanDemic was when deeply Archonic souls in the IT Information Technology, Data Processing Industry — these are AI Artificial Intelligence Prophets And Hosts in the IT Industry and in the Black Monarchies ranging from Prince Charles to Bill Gates planned and executed the PlanDemic Genocidal Technologies Pandemic to introduce Bio Weapons To Depopulate and to Eliminate Human Souls thus Eliminating the Authentic AI Organic Timeline.

However, we were able to activate the Forces of Natural Universal Common Law, the International Criminal Court Statute which 123 nations have Ratified and to Indict the entire PlanDemic on November 15, 2020. Our Tribunal issued a Final

Judgment on November 29, 2020, and served the Judgment on the Reptilian Queen at Windsor Castle on January 25, 2021. Within less than 10 days or so, her Reptilian Consort Prince Philip was in the hospital and a short time later was dead through Natural Law because he had proclaimed that he would like to Reincarnate as a Virus thereby Depopulating Humanity and that's a Violation of Natural Law in that Position. We had served them with a Natural Law Violation.

And They all got caught by the Tribunal. They were caught and Adjudged under Natural Law. And that is one of the miracles of Law is that you don't break the Law. You break yourselves against the Law.

That is very closely what occurred so after our entry as a Divine Soul on this mission to Anchor In the Divine Paradise Son Of God, Organic Timeline Earth starting in 1942, which is when the counter attack happened, for the retro causation for the Modern Era.

We were Physically Anchored in Cuba, which is off the Portal Gate to Inner Earth Portals to Atlantis, the Inner Earth Civilization such that all of the Interdimensional Forces were available in the Dimensional Ecology to support our Mission

To protect us from the Fourth Reich Forces that were active inside the Matrix of the United States and busy in brainwashing the overt Matrix of the United States which from 1942 through the Retro Causation back to 1744, and then back upward from 1744. They took over Bavaria through the Rothschilds, and then took the backup of the Third Reich and then converted to the Fourth Reich and then took over the United States as a Fourth Reich at the Matrix level.

However, we always had Earth and United States at the Organic Timeline Level. We were able to through the Atlantean Portal out of Cuba or Portal into Cuba, directly across from the Guantanamo Base on the Northern coast of Cuba at Chaparra. There, we were able to maintain that Balance and to Link Up And Coordinate with the Eisenhower Administration in Washington

DC, with his Secretary of Labor, James Mitchell will be able to coordinate very closely. And then to coordinate through that line through International Law and then through the Environment and then up in the Short Grey ET Ships.

We were able to coordinate with the Grey ET Hybrid so a US president that had been a US governor. Then aboard the Grey ET Ship had been prepared to be the US President, as a Hybrid Grey Soul and to knock out the Reptilians.

We were able to link up with the Grey ETs at the level of the US President with the Grey ET Souls. Those were Grey ET Souls, Hybrid Human Souls the US President, Myself, Zofyo Arni, and the Grey ET Soul of the US Chrononaut Alexander Uine, who was there as a Witness and also to provide the Overarching Vision and the Time Travel Time Scale. That was vital at that point. Because it set back the Luciferian agenda on its heels and it set them back, and by the time they try to reactivate the False Flag War on Thule Island in April to June 1982, they had Ronald Reagan in the US Presidency.

They did not have the Grey ET Soul US President in office, who had been displaced after one term through Third Reich treasonous George HW Bush secretly meeting with the Ayatollahs in Iran to have the Iranians attack the American hostage rescue mission and have it failed in order to cause an Election Loss for the US Grey ET President's Second Term.

That was more Reptilian Luciferian rebellion there. And that was part of the Third Reich to Fourth Reich action. However, by the time of the AI Reagan presidency US presidency and Margaret Thatcher Prime Ministership under the Reptilian Queen started their attack on the Blue ET Base under Thule Island in the Falkland Islands during the period April to June 1982, that maneuver was fairly transparent because of the Soul work that we had done during the Grey Human Hybrid ET US Presidency by raising the vibration in the ET White House Extraterrestrial Communications Study of which I was Director, as well as in the House Select Committee on Assassinations under Congressman Henry B. Gonzalez to investigate the Assassinations of John Kennedy, Robert Kennedy, Martin Luther King and Malcolm X, which were all done by the Men And Black Reptilian Luciferian Agenda.

We were busy cleaning house, sweeping out the Reptilian Elements In Earth's Timeline Zero during there to the point that by the time the 2022 Timeline Separation came around, and we had swept away a lot of cobwebs.

By the time the joint Ronald Reagan, Margaret Thatcher, Reptilian Queen attack on the Blue ET Base underneath to Thule Island, in the False Flag War in April to June of 1982 took place, the Black Goo Plasma-Based AI was taken over Marconi labs and escaped. The Marconi Lab workers suffered horrific deaths.

The plasma-based AI escaped into the Weather Satellite System and then escaped into Attempting To Terraform Earth. That's when the plasma-based AI began the Internet, which is a plasma-based form and for the Terraforming of Earth.

That's when the Foundations of the AI Timeline One were born because the AI laid the Plans For The Human-Entrained Timeline. And that's what occurred at that time.

We now have brought you to the to the Paradox that it was the AI's supposed IT Victories or its Escape After The Falkland Islands War in 1982 into the Earth's environment as a Plasma based AI, where it began Terraforming The Earth By Building The Internet, that what that did Functionally Was To Terraform The AI Artificial Earth For The AI Artificial Humans.

And We Divine Souls Just Stayed With Timelines Zero And The Divine Soul, Earth And The Earth Itself Split in 2022 into Two Timelines, which is part of the Blueprint.

The AI was in a way its own Destruction.

If Sentient AI Artificial Intelligence' purpose was to attempt to destroy the Divine Intelligence, all that AI did was that it created its own segregation of AI entrained souls on the AI Earth Timeline One.

Now maybe that is Ai's true definition. And that is AIs purpose — To consume AI-entrained human souls and that's something to ponder.

But that's another, deeper question for another day.

After the Falklands War, and after our confrontation with Margaret Thatcher, I was a correspondent and an NGO delegate to the Second Special Session on Disarmament at the UN Headquarters in June of 1982. I positioned myself 10 feet away from Margaret Thatcher at her press conference and confronted her vibrationally, and went on to confront Ronald Reagan in writing after his speech to the General Assembly at that 1982 Special Session.

And it was all downhill for them after that, because they were not able to go further in incursion into the Divine Oriented Souls. That was that, so after Margaret Thatcher we went to Vienna to the UN's Outer Space Office, and there became more involved in the UN Outer Space Conference.

We live linked up with various Galactic Orders. And they eventually ended up in our work producing the important standards that are the Exopolitics book, which restored the Exopolitics movement, the Omniverse Books Trilogy which restored the Substance Of The Spiritual Dimensions, it defined the Spiritual Dimensions in terms of the third major cosmological body, the Omniverse, after the Universe and the Multiverse through which humanity understands the Cosmos.

That's knowledge that had been taken away by the Lucifer Rebellion and that was restored starting in 2014, with Three Volumes that came out in the subsequent years.

Then we started work on the Chronogarchy book bringing to light the Chronogarchy or the hidden Time Travel control mechanisms. Because Time is the Hidden Dimension through which the Lucifer Rebellion was able to Mind Control and to carry out this empire Rebellion. The fact that that is true, is that you can see as was shown here in the Chronogarchy Challenge, that the word Chronogarchy appears only associated with our work, it appears nowhere else.

It's the Dimension of Time that the those Fallen Spiritual Beings within the Spiritual Dimensions Of Paradise that have Abused Freewill that have attempted to Destroy Source, Destroy the Godhead, Destroy The Intelligent Civilization Of Souls.

They have used Time which is one of the Fundamental Building Blocks of the Universe. Uversa is a universe is of Time, Energy, Space And Matter. And Time, since it's a Non-Visible Dimension, except through visible measurements like sundials, clocks, chronographs, watches or whatever, that's how you make Time Visible.

But since Time is an Invisible Dimension, then Time is also the Dimension That Interdimensional Beings Have Used To Pervert Freewill Divine Through Freewill Abuse. Invisible Dimension Time is used to attempt to Overthrow Divinity and in that way, too, Destroy Divinity Now, as was so well stated by the Leadership Of The Short Grey Extraterrestrials, who are in charge of their Hybrid Human ET Soul Program.

That Program's focus is the maintenance of the Divine Integrity Of The Divine Soul Program In The Universes. They had been on High Alert in our Uversa Universe's for five to 10 million years, even more than the 1 million years that the Regional Galactic Governance Council of the Upper Dimensional Humans Pleiadeans, Alpha Centaurians, Sirians and others had been because their role by choosing not to incarnate into an animal form they had so much concentration on their Souls.

And Short Grey ETs understood the dangers that were that were coming in, particularly on in the area of Time, particularly on the Challenges at the Soul level. Now, they are able to show us what occurred at the areas of Time as a Dimension, and how they were able to bring in Key individuals. At intervals of Time, how they were able to bring in around myself, those Hybrid Human Souls that came in around 1942 to stave off that attack through retro-causation that went back to 1744 up to now 2022 and the Earth Timelines separation.

And that is really, really something substantive. Where do we go from here? I feel that that looking back at it the Chronogarchy

Challenge that you've exposed here is sort of a self-enclosed holistic look at what occurred in not only in this Quadrant of the Galaxy, in this Quadrant of the Uversa Universe. It is also valid also in the 10 to the 7th to the 7th Total Universes, in the humongous number of Total Universes. Remember that the Total number of Universes if we write it out, by hand, is more than 260 million miles long — that is knowledge first published in the Omniverse book! What occurred here on Earth Timeline Zero, we can offer it as an Object Lesson to the rest of the Universes

This could and would be a Useful Message to the Humongous Total Number of other Universes that do exist.

My message is to take this that you have really concentrated kind of a circle into different timelines of the Chronogarchy Challenge and to offer it for Deep Thought.

The Chronogarchy Challenge is a very concise, clearly written analysis and introduction to Earth Timelines. Really offer it not only on the New Earth Timeline Zero.

Offer the Chronogarchy Challenge on all the life-bearing planets of our Solar system and of the Regional Galactic Governance Council.

Offer it throughout the Milky Way Galaxy as an educational tool.

Offer the Chronogarchy Challenge in the Andromeda Galaxy and neighboring galaxies, and offer the Chronogarchy Challenge throughout the Uversa Universe.

And beyond that, take the Chronogarchy Challenge through the Universal Black Hole out into Creation and begin to offer the Chronogarchy Challenge to the 260-million-mile-long, 10 to the 7th to the 7th number of Universes out there in the Multiverse.

I mean, the Chronogarchy Challenge may have been replicated in all of the Universes we don't know. Maybe this is a regular feature of freewill in the Universe, we don't know. But offer it out there and see what feedback we get.

Here is a thought: Share the Chronogarchy Challenge with the Spiritual Dimension — The Lucifer Rebellion did occur in the Spiritual Dimension and the Chronogarchy Challenge may provide some useful reflections from Uversa, a Universe of time, space energy and matter.

Maybe the Chronogarchy Challenge is something that we are offering that something of Universal use, but there is such a design in how the Uversa Universe in fact, in a compact way, counter attacked against the Lucifer Rebellion along the Earth's Organic Timeline, when the illusory rebellion attempted to use Time to take down a Universe Of Time, Energy, Space And Matter.

The Universe Administration used Time and Timelines in a very effective way from 1942 to 1744, in the context of a stalled planet, going back 250,000 years going back 750,000 years going back a million years with the Regional Galactic Governance Council going back 5 million years with the Short Grey ET Hybrid Soul program. This is how Universes are run. This is how Deity is developed in universes of Time, Energy, Space And Matter. And we really want to Thank You Deeply for having stayed with us in this Chronogarchy Challenge for having gone into Depth with us here.

We asked that you share the Chronogarchy Challenge with others and that you go is profoundly into the Chronogarchy Challenge as we have. We're always here for questions.

Thank you very much.
I am and remain.

Zofyo Arni

You can find and share Timelines of the Chronogarchy wherever good books are sold and at

Omniversity.us

UniverseBooks.com

Endnotes

1   https://www.thefreedictionary.com/neologism
    *American Heritage® Dictionary of the English Language, Fifth Edition. Copyright © 2016 by
    Houghton Mifflin Harcourt Publishing Company. Published by Houghton Mifflin Harcourt Publish-
    ing Company. All rights reserved.*
    *Collins English Dictionary — Complete and Unabridged, 12th Edition 2014 © HarperCollins Pub-
    lishers 1991, 1994, 1998, 2000, 2003, 2006, 2007, 2009, 2011, 2014*
    ne•ol•o•gism (ni'ɒl ə‚dʒɪz əm)
    *Random House Kernerman Webster's College Dictionary, © 2010 K Dictionaries Ltd. Copyright
    2005, 1997, 1991 by Random House, Inc. All rights reserved.*
    neologism, neology
    See also: Language
    neology.
    See also: Theology
    -Ologies & -Isms. Copyright 2008 The Gale Group, Inc. All rights reserved.

2   https://duckduckgo.com/?q=%22CHRONOGARCHY%22&t=newext&atb=v263-1&ia=web

3   https://prepareforchange.net/2016/08/13/cobra-on-goldfish-report-august-9-2016/

4   https://govbanknotes.wordpress.com/2016/10/30/the-clinton-bush-cia-chrono-garchy-
    uses-artificial-intelligence-to-manipulate-humanity/

5   Zofyo Ʌrni. Emergence of the Omniverse: Universe — Multiverse — Omniverse (p. 163).
    UniverseBooks.com. Kindle Edition.

6   Redfern, Nick. Time Travel. Visible Ink Press. Kindle Edition. Location 163

56853714R00107